LETTERS
IN A
GRAVE

LETTERS
IN A
GRAVE

GEORGE KANAWATY

LETTERS IN A GRAVE

iUniverse books may be ordered through booksellers or by contacting:

iUniverse
1663 Liberty Drive
Bloomington, IN 47403
www.iuniverse.com
844-349-9409

ISBN: 978-1-6632-3827-6 (sc)
ISBN: 978-1-6632-3826-9 (e)

Library of Congress Control Number: 2022906574

Print information available on the last page.

iUniverse rev. date: 04/11/2022

Dedication

To Georgette, Savannah, Thomas, Dylan and Trevor.

Author's Note

I had the good fortune of having had an international career. This led me to live in ten different countries and to visit many parts of the world. The biggest reward, however, had been to meet persons of varied backgrounds and life-stories to tell. While the characters in this novel are fictious, the events mentioned take place in non-fiction settings. They are based on interviews with persons, I met, such as that with Zine Hamilton, mentioned in this novel, who a couple of decades ago, at 106 years of age, gave me an account of his arrival to Canada as an immigrant in 1906. My own experiences, such as witnessing the Vietnam war, when I was stationed in next door Cambodia, provided an additional input. Other historical events, some of which are little known to the general public, add more to the settings for this novel.

Chapter One

Paul Hamilton looked again at the accumulated mail on the side board. Among the various letters, was a bunch of ribbon-tied envelopes delivered by the funeral home. They must be sympathy cards and notices of donations made in his mother's memory, he figured. For three days, they have been lying there, but he had no desire to read them.

One more unpleasant task awaited him. Disposing of his mother's belongings. For ten days he has been finding one excuse after another, to postpone doing anything about it. For her personal belongings, he could seek the help of a distant cousin living in the city, and with an assistance from the cleaning lady they could sort these out for him. He would rather have them accomplish this task in his absence. However, personal belongings went beyond clothes and toiletries. There were papers, photos, books, all stored in a room, that his late mother sometimes referred to as her sanctuary. He had to go through these himself. That room, had a comfortable armchair, a sofa, a shelved cabinet that held her books and then there was her desk.

On top of that desk sat her computer and beside it, a framed picture of her, taken some thirty years earlier holding him as a baby. He recalled how as a young boy he had asked his mother what was in the desk drawers, while attempting to open one, and how she immediately stopped him and gave him a lecture about respecting the privacy of others. He never made another attempt to go through her drawers since. Today, he will go through her papers, to decide which ones to keep and which to discard. He will do that, after paying her a visit at the cemetery. Two weeks had passed since her funeral, and he had been to visit her only once, since.

It was a beautiful Saturday morning in Toronto. Paul drove to the Mount Pleasant cemetery, stopped by the flower shop by the gate, and picked a red rose, his mother's favorite.

Established in 1876, on the outskirts of the city, at the time, Mount Pleasant gradually expanded. At present, it occupied 200 acres right in the heart of Toronto and accommodated over 160,000 deceased residents. Mount Pleasant is known to be a peaceful and a beautiful place of rolling hills, vast expanses of lawn with a multitude of rare trees, shrubs, flowers, water fountains and occasional monuments. This landscape, accommodates kilometers of pathways, and paved roads. To a casual visitor, Mount Pleasant, looks like a huge botanical garden, with the headstones thrown in as a sideline decoration. The graves themselves, ranged from simple slabs on the ground, to headstones and large mausoleums. The head stones, wore different colors; black, pink, grey and green. They also bore writings in several languages predominantly English but also Chinese, Hebrew, Russian and other languages.

Paul headed towards a newer section of the cemetery, reserved for the cremated. On his way he passed several cemetery workers. With their green uniforms, they operated various machines, big lawn mowers, machines that collected fallen leaves, swept, and cleaned the pathways or watered the flower beds. The workers were also performing other tasks, trimming trees and hedges, planting flowers, and emptying trash bins. On his way, he also crossed path with joggers, cyclists, people strolling or even walking their pets. There were also students of art, trying their hand at sketching or painting landscapes.

Paul's destination was a wall covered with distinct tiles. One tile bore the inscription "Anne Hamilton 1922-1994 For Ever Remembered" A painted red rose featured below that inscription. Behind that tile, lay an urn holding his mother's ashes. Paul replaced the old withered rose; he had left five days earlier, with the new one he had just brought. After a few minutes of silent meditation, he sat on the lawn.

There he was, thirty years old, with an eight years old failed marriage behind him. Facing him were the remains of the person he loved most of all; his mentor, his counsellor, and the home maker in a family that, at present, had dwindled to him alone. His father "Jeff", died several years earlier and was buried at his family's lot in Kingston, his home town. Jeff worked at a large insurance company in Toronto. His job was to sell insurance policies across the Provence of Ontario. This entailed frequent travels to various parts of the Provence. It also involved him entertaining potential customers on the golf course or taking them out on pleasure junkets. When Jeff changed jobs to become an assessor of insurance claims, that again required a certain amount of travelling. As a result, Paul did not see as much of his father, as he would have liked. Still, Jeff provided him and his mother, with a comfortable home and supported his education, often showing interest in his scholastic achievements.

It was his mother Anne, who devoted herself to him. Despite the demands of her government job, she was always there to guide him through his schooling and to answer any question he threw at her. It was shortly after he was born, that his parents bought their home. A bungalow style old house situated in a good residential area of Toronto. It was spacious enough for Paul to have his own good-sized room from a very young age, and for his mother to have a room of her own as well, which she called; "her sanctuary". Anne made sure that their home was properly kept, that a good meal always awaited them at dinner time, and if Jeff was not there, she would invariably introduce young Paul to arts, music, humanity, even world affairs.

He remembered how since a young age she would recount to him over dinner, the life of a classical music composer, followed by playing some of his compositions after dinner. Thanks to her he became acquainted with many classical composers. On other occasions, with him at her side, they went through volumes of impressionist paintings, introducing him to the works of Monet, Renoir, Van Gogh, and Pissarro among others. As he grew up, topics at the dinner table, changed to the root causes of poverty in the world, to local and national politics to the events surrounding the Second World War, to employment promotion, and to reconstruction efforts going on in Europe and elsewhere.

Anne worked at the Employment Bureau of the Government of Ontario. Her job was to find employment for job seekers. She was known to be thorough, fair, but also a no-nonsense sort of person. Among her colleagues at work, she was well liked and respected.

When Paul finished university, he joined a company in the city, as an information technology professional. A job that matched his interest in the growing area of computer use. During his teen years, he had dated several girls, but invariably wavered when it came to marriage prospects. On such occasions, he sought his mother's opinion. She readily gave him the pros and cons, in each case, which he appreciated, as he often only saw the positive side of each girl. At twenty-two, he met Dorothy, a year older and a colleague at work. A beautiful girl with a bubbly personality and the life of every party. They dated for a couple of months, before falling madly in love. He wanted her to meet his mother. Over dinner, that evening, Dorothy monopolized the conversation, leaving little room for him or his mother to express any opinions. Over coffee, and much to Anne's surprise, Dorothy disclosed the preparations she was making for her upcoming marriage to "Darling Paul". It was only then, that Anne discovered, that Paul had already proposed to her. When Dorothy left, Paul, bubbling all over enthusiastically about his new bride to be, asked his mother what she thought of her. He expected a non-equivocal endorsement. Deep in her heart, Anne felt that Dorothy was not the right person for her son. She worried, however, that she could lose both her son and his prospective wife if she gave a negative answer:

- Just make sure, that she is the right person you want to spend your life with. You are mature enough Paul. It is you who must make that decision.

After the euphoria of the honeymoon faded, it was not long before Paul discovered that their interests in life were widely different. Dorothy wanted to party as much as possible. Housekeeping was not a priority, nor was bringing up children. She considered herself too young to be encumbered with getting pregnant and raising children. Her drinking and smoking increased with time, and he was unable to engage her in any meaningful discussion, like the ones he used to have with his mother.

Two years later, they came to the inevitable conclusion. They were simply not a good match and resolved to an amiable divorce. That experience shook Paul badly. He wondered, whether he was the marrying type, and for three years thereafter, he kept to himself. Eventually he dated again, going out with women within his age bracket, but after a third or a fourth date, his dating companion invariably asked him if he had serious intentions. That was a signal for him to end a relation. He was not ready for another marriage and another possible failure. Now with his mother gone, he felt a bit lost. He missed her terribly.

When he returned home that day, Paul went to his mother's sanctuary. There was no point going through the bookshelf containing her books or her music collection. He went straight to her desk. He opened the top left drawer. It contained bank statements and tax slips, the second drawer had several files; one file contained her graduation certificate, another his father's death certificate, and a copy of his will, a third had the deed of the house and the receipts for major appliances bought. He turned his attention to the right-hand drawers. The top drawer contained the usual writing material, pens, a container for stamps, a pencil sharpener, a few cables for her computer and a key, which he did not recognize. He closed it, and opened the second drawer. It contained a large brown envelope full of pictures. They were not arranged in an album or in any discernable order. He went quickly through some of them. There was a picture of her probably at fifteen or thereabouts with long pony tail hair, another was her wedding picture, then there were lots of pictures showing Anne in various places often with friends, with Jeff or with cousins who lived in far-away places like New York, Oregon, and Vancouver. He recognized some faces, having met them on rare occasions.

He closed that drawer and tried opening the last bottom drawer. It was locked. He tried the key found in the top drawer. It worked. Inside that drawer, he found a smaller brown envelope with pictures. and behind it was a box. He opened the small envelope it contained pictures of a person he did not recognize, a youthful young man, others showed him with his mother in her younger days in Canada somewhere. There were pictures taken later in life, of both

7

his mother and that person by the Eiffel Tower in Paris, but most of the remaining pictures showed that person alone and were taken in various places.

He returned the pictures to their envelope, opened the drawer wider, pulled out the box and opened it. It contained a bundle of letters tied with an elastic band and a black leather notebook. The letters were addressed to Mrs. Anne Hamilton, his mother. He was curious about the notebook. Was that a diary that his mother kept ?

Chapter Two

Paul went quickly through the letters. All had the same handwriting on the envelopes with one exception. He picked that letter and started reading it.

10 April 1992

Dear Mrs. Hamilton,

My name is Julie Wien. It is with much regret and deep sadness that I write to inform you that my beloved father Hans Wien passed away yesterday at the Northumberland Hills hospital in Cobourg, where I work.

A week before going to the hospital, he made me promise that in case of his death, I was to destroy your letters to him. Letters that he had kept locked and greatly cherished. Having heard so much about you, I confess that in carrying out his wish, I read them beforehand and took great comfort in knowing that his love for you, was reciprocated. A few years back, he bought a plot in Mount Pleasant cemetery, in Toronto, where he wanted to be buried. He used to ride his bike there in earlier years and always thought of it as the most peaceful place he knew.

In accordance with his wish, his funeral will be held in private with only close family and friends invited to attend. The service will take place at 4 p.m., next Wednesday the 14th at the cemetery's funeral center. If you can attend, I will be honored to meet the person I always took as my foster mother.

With much affection.

Julie

Paul was in a daze. His mother exchanged love letters with someone called Hans!

He felt that he was reading the end, before knowing the story. His mother never revealed such a relation to anybody; not to him nor, he supposed, to his father. He now, not only has a name for that person, a certain Hans, but also pictures of him. No doubt, the extent of this relation will be revealed in the letters before him. His mother's diary may also shed additional light. He settled in the armchair to go through them. On top of the pile, was the letter that arrived last. He began to read it.

3 April 1992

Anne, my dearest,

Forgive my handwriting. No matter how hard I try, my shaky hands do not always obey my command. Apart from other ailments, I realize now that I suffer badly from a chronic disease for which there is no cure. It is called old age. Do not worry; my love for you keeps me going. I continue to dream of the sheer happiness, we could have experienced, had we spent our lives together. Got married at a younger age and raised a family. When my time in this world is up, my dearest, the memories of our happy times together will always keep me alive wherever I end.

Julie just arrived to take me to the hospital, my doctor's dictate, I have no idea when I will be able to write again. I kiss you fondly, in my imagination, now and as I have always done over the years.

Hans

Paul put that letter down. He turned his attention to the diary. The first entry was in 1943.

15 May 1943,

Yesterday I turned twenty- one. After much reflection, I decided to start a diary. What will I write? Only important events that I can read again later on in life. I do not want to commit to writing daily or on specific dates. Important events in my life, will be what will prompt me to write. I want to put on paper feelings that sometimes I cannot share with others. This diary will be restricted. Nobody should read it or even know of its existence. It is mine and mine alone.

Ever since my young age, I was intrigued by my family name. The name Hamilton is as English as it gets. Yet, my parents speak English with a pronounced accent. In this country, people do not hide their ethnic background. They often refer to themselves as English Canadians or French Canadians. Other ethnic groups organize relevant community activities. The Chinese have a China Town in Toronto, where even the names of the streets are written in both English and Chinese, The Greeks tend to cluster in the Danforth neighborhood of the city with lots of Greek restaurants; and so on. My mother once mentioned that she and father were originally from Syria. My classmates always took me as an English Canadian given my Hamilton name.

I never claimed otherwise.

If my parents were Syrian, how did they acquire such an English name? My father Zine, often laughed at my query, and would give me an evasive answer. A month ago, I pressed him again, and he decided that I was now mature enough to get the full story.

His original first name was Zain el Abdeen, but he was called Zain for short. He was born in what was called "The Great Syria", a part of the Ottoman Empire. Great Syria, encompassed, what is nowadays known as Syria and Lebanon, put together. His family was poor. His father owned and worked half an acre of land, and raised four sheep and some chicken to survive.

Life under the Ottoman Empire was precarious. The Empire's territory at one time, extended from Arabia and the middle East to parts of Europe, including the Balkans, Greece, Bulgaria, and a part of the Crimea. This brought it into occasional armed confrontation with both the Austro- Hungarian and the Russian empires. In addition, internal dissent, in Greece, Bulgaria, the Arab region meant that it was in constant armed conflict. That Empire was also badly in debt.

As a result, supplies to the army were not always regular nor guaranteed. Garrison commanders, were sometimes left on their own, to figure out a way to feed their troops. In addition to occasionally raiding the countryside, confiscating crops, poultry, and livestock, they also descended on the cities and villages of the empire, conscripting adults into the army, to compensate for losses suffered in combat, by disease, or by desertion. Nobody really knew the number of soldiers in that multi-ethnic Ottoman army.

It was at the age of six, that young Zain, one day, heard his father arguing with soldiers outside their dwelling. He was trying to convince them to spare his four sheep. Two shots were fired, his father was dead, and the sheep were gone. His mother succumbed to a disease four years later. He was ten years old, when he became an orphan. An uncle took him under his wings. That uncle had two acres of land to which was added the half acre that came with Zain. He assisted the uncle in working the land and herding the small flock of sheep that the uncle owned.

His aunt lived in fear, that as Zain came of age, he could be drafted in the Ottoman's army. One day, her brother, who had immigrated to "America" years earlier, returned for a visit to the old country, and to his own family. His aunt conveyed to her brother, her fears. Could he help by finding a job for Zain in "America"? Zain remember that uncle asking him in a teasing manner:

–   Zain. Do you want to come to America?

He nodded yes without knowing what this America was, except that the better dressed uncle, with money to spend, represented a place where life was better than his village. It was only later, that he realized that the uncle's America was in fact Canada. At that time, in Syria, every place far away, in the north or south of the Atlantic was called America.

A year passed, before money could be secured to buy him a passage. He still remembered the boat's name. It was the S/S Alesia steamship. In 1906, at sixteen years of age, he joined some two hundred people boarding that one- class ship in Beirut. It had arrived from Alexandria with passengers, stopped in Beirut to take more passengers before heading to Constantinople, Salonica and reaching Marseille a week later, where all 800 passengers on board disembarked. They were tested for Glaucoma, those who had it were not authorized to continue the journey. Two days later, the remaining passengers, including Zain, embarked again destined for one of the two next ports of calls; Halifax in Canada, then New York in the United States. Zain disembarked in Halifax, as he had been told to do.

The immigration lines in Halifax were long. Two immigration officers screened the migrants accompanied by several interpreters. One officer asked the questions, the second recorded the answers and issued a name tag. When two hours later, his turn came, he gave his name as he was asked to do. This was too complicated for the officer to comprehend. He was asked to repeat it, and to pronounce it slowly.

"Zain el Abdeen"., he answered. Still unable to comprehend that name, the officer told his colleague "Put him down as Zine".

- What is your family name?
- Shankahlou, came his answer.

What an impossible name said the officer impatiently.

- Where are you going?
- To my uncle.
- Where is your uncle?
- in a place called Hamilton.

The officer looked at his colleague and said:

- Put him down as Hamilton.

So, a tag was issued stating his name as Zine Hamilton. A medical exam followed mainly to ascertain that he was free from Tuberculosis. He was then given a train ticket from Halifax to Hamilton.

I asked my father what happened next. He smiled:

- Do you really want to know?
- absolutely
- My uncle ran a general store in Hamilton selling everything from axle grease to kitchen utensils, oil lamps and hardware tools. He also stocked edible products like flour, sugar, rice, corn, selling them by the bag at reduced prices. My job was to clean the store every day, cart the goods in and out of the store, and do various errands. For sleeping, I was given a cot in the store room, I had my meals with my uncle and his family for free and received a modest stipend.

A few years later, I learnt the secrets of the trade, and spoke English reasonably well. When I became twenty-three or thereabouts, I decided to strike it on my own. By that time, I had saved enough money to allow me to buy a horse, a mule, camping equipment, kitchen utensils and some tools; which my uncle sold them to me at a discount. I had shared my idea with him and he encouraged me to follow it through.

I loaded my camping equipment and most of the goods on the mule and some others on the horse, which I rode, and headed north to the Indigenous Indian and Eskimo land. It took me almost a month to reach the first village far north, populated by indigenous Indians. It was early spring, a period recommended by my uncle and the snow had not completely melted. I traded my kitchen utensils including knives, some hardware; axes, hammers, nails, and the like for fur that the indigenous Indian population had trapped from various wild animals. These included fox, beavers, grisly and black bears. They suggested other villages that I may wish to visit as well. Three months later I was back in Hamilton loaded with furs. My uncle helped me sell them and I made a fortune. I repeated the experience in the fall with two mules and continued trading with the indigenous people but I had other ambitions. I wanted to venture further north, and reach eskimo land. I accomplished this a year later, and after a long and hard trek I reached my destination, traded with the eskimos, and returned this time, with the fur of arctic fox, Polar bear, and mink. These brought in much higher returns. I continued these trading expeditions, for a few years.

By then, I had made enough money to allow me to go and visit a distant uncle who had recently immigrated to New York. There I met his eighteen years old daughter, fresh from the old country, she had been barely a year in America.

I proposed and she became your mother.

The rest you know, I made the rounds of the retailers in the city and its surroundings. I found out their needs. I then I started a wholesale business importing merchandise from the United States and other parts of Canada, selling them to retailers at discount prices.

Listening to my father, made me realize for the first time what he went through to provide us with a comfortable life. There was no reason for me, to conceals my Syrian origins anymore.

2 June 1944

A big day, I just graduated from Toronto University with a Bachelor degree in arts. This was not a one-day celebration event. First, my parents took me out to a luxurious restaurant, then several classmates organized various parties at their homes where I enjoyed myself to the fullest dancing and meeting new faces, a couple of men asked me out. I accepted one invitation from Bill. Will that lead to something serious; we shall see. Listening to all the depressing news from the war front, I sometimes feel guilty enjoying myself.

I need to think of getting a job. Now that the studies are over, I have tons of spare time, cannot continue to be idle, or be a financial burden on my family. My father, who retired years ago is ailing. It bothers me to see him slowing down and holding on to a walker to go places. Mother too is worried about him. May God grant them a long life.

19 September 1944

I did not think I will write again so soon. But next Monday I start a job with the Ontario Employment Bureau. My first job! Exciting news, worth writing about.

Will know more about my exact duties on Monday. Very happy, a bit apprehensive.

2 September 1945

Wonderful news. The war is over. There are demonstrations in the streets. We were given the day off, but instead we celebrated with a drink at the office at precisely 11 a.m., the time the fighting officially stopped. There were hugs, kisses, and tears as someone distributed to us small Canadian flags. I went out with my flag to the street, kissing and being kissed by many, unknown to me. One big spontaneous street celebration. People singing "long way to Tipperary" and "God save the King". Others joining hands in disjointed dances. A great and unforgettable time.

There had been a lot of talk at the office and for a long time, that when this war is over our work load will increase dramatically as we will be expected to find jobs for the thousands of demobilized soldiers. Cannot wait to start doing so. Feel so happy, wish my father was alive to hear this news.

Chapter Three

3 June 1946

I had a glance at my entry in 1944, where I mentioned dating Bill. Well, that relation lasted only a few weeks, several other dating engagements followed but no one impressed me as a candidate husband. I guess I must wait longer. No hurry.

I continue to enjoy myself going out with men. I need company, and I find them useful as partners for dancing or for other social events. So far, I turned down two marriage proposals. Better wait, than being sorry.

I had a strange experience at the office today. All job seekers start by filling a form giving their personal data, before being called for an interview. When I looked at the application form before me, I was surprised. The name was Hans Wien, nationality German. What is a German person doing in Canada and the nerve to be asking for work ! With all the tens of thousands of

Canadians killed and maimed during the war fighting the Germans, here is one of them wanting our help for a job in this country.

I called him over, preparing to be expeditious. In a very polite manner and after some prodding on my part, he told me that he had just been released from a camp for German prisoners of war. His application form showed that he had dropped out of university education before finishing his third year. The University he went to was quoted as Basel University in Switzerland. When I quizzed him about that, he said he was studying economics there, but circumstances forced him to leave. He wanted me to overlook that segment in the application, saying that he would be just as glad to find any manual job. Why don't you return to Germany, now that the war is over, I asked, to which he answered that he has no family or home to return to. He had been in Canada for the last three years, albeit in the camp. Even then, he was allowed to do manual work on a farm. He got to meet Canadians, who were all kind to him, particularly when they got to know him better. He was desperate to settle in this country. Once more he begged me to help him.

This story, had several gaps which intrigued me. Why did he go to a Swiss university when he could have attended a German one? How and where was he taken prisoner? I posed a few questions, but got evasive answers. Apart from German, Hans was fluent in English and French, a definite asset for him in Quebec. Should I help? That will entail contacting colleagues in another Provence, something that falls beyond my line of duties. Faced with his courteous pleas, I reluctantly told him that I will see what can be done to help, though I could not promise anything, I asked him to pass again in ten days' time.

2 October 1947

My life has settled to a routine, regular working hours, active social life including going to concerts and plays, alone if there are no willing partners. Funny, I often find more women willing to join me on such occasions than men.

Work has been stressful with hundreds, if not thousands, of demobilized soldiers seeking jobs, but it has also been challenging and at times heart breaking, trying to find work for handicapped veterans. I needed a break, so this summer, I drove to Quebec, spent a week touring the Laurentians and sampling Quebec cuisine.

I enjoyed staying at a small hotel by the lake, in St. Adele, making this a base from which I took drives to various other lakes and villages. I should brush on my French, which was quite rusty when I tried to use it there.

On my return, I found a letter from Hans Wien thanking me for my help in finding him a job as a bell boy at the Queen Elizabeth Hotel in Montreal. I had forgotten all about him. He mentioned that he had applied for Canadian residency as a prelude to citizenship, but was told that it was a difficult and a lengthy process, particularly since he was not legally admitted to Canada as an immigrant. I wrote back wishing him well and asking him to keep me informed of his progress in life.

16 April 1950

My mother keeps pressing me to get married. I told her that none of the men I dated impressed me. Most, seem to have three preoccupations, which, in descending order were, the ice hockey and football results, their exploits on the golf course comes next and then the stock market. Listening to them, I usually nod approval of whatever they were saying; occasionally pretending interest, but inside of me I would be bored to death. My mother said that I was too picky, she wanted to see grandchildren before she died. Had I received marriage proposals lately. I told her that love expressions and marriage proposals made by some men, were sometimes so crude, that they were repulsive. "You will never meet somebody like me" or "I love you like you will never believe it" as for proposals, they were sometimes expressed so badly like "Let us do it honey", or "With your salary and mine we can have a great life together".

My mother told me she cannot understand our generation when we insist on love before marriage. Look at me, she added. I barely knew your father when we got married. As time went by, we learnt to smooth our differences and love developed gradually. I saw no point in arguing with her, gave her a hug and assured her that I was working on it.

23

During the last couple of years, I received a few letters from Hans. He took it to heart to keep me informed as I had suggested earlier to him out of politeness. He keeps repeating how grateful he is to me. It makes me feel good. In one letter he tells me that as a new comer, he was put on the night shift, which suited him best. It allowed him to enroll in Sir George Williams University in Montreal as a regular morning student studying accounting. He had money transferred from a bank account he held in Switzerland to cover his tuition. That raised my eyebrows, this fellow is full of mystery. I am curious and wish to find more about him. He has solved his residency problems as he is now on a student visa. I congratulated him and urged him to keep in touch.

25 June 1952

My curiosity regarding Hans got the most of me. I wrote suggesting him coming to Toronto for the day. I hinted that I wanted to know more about him as this, may enable me to help him better. If he was able to arrive to Toronto by noon or earlier, I could arrange a picnic lunch. Am I glad I took this initiative. I spent a fascinating day.

I met Hans at the Toronto train station. We took the subway to Ontario Place, where we found a quiet place by the lake to spread our lunch. I had brought some sandwiches and a couple of apples. For drinks, he opted for beer instead of wine and bought two cans. He also brought me a bottle of maple syrup and a box of maple candies.

I told him that he should stop addressing me as Miss Hamilton and just call me Anne. He blushed, apologized, and said that in his culture calling a person by his or her first name, is reserved for intimate friends, otherwise it shows a sign of disrespect.

I told him that if we were to become friends then we need to know everything about each other. I started by telling him about my Syrian roots and my hobbies.

After much hesitation, he relayed to me his life story.

He came from a distinguished family that lived in old Prussia, before German unification. Although he was born in a village called Gaffken, they soon moved to Dresden, as his father Wilhelm Wien, a well known and highly respected Physicist, became a professor at the Dresden University of Technology. His father died in 1928. As an only child, his mother, a strong-willed woman doted on him. They led a comfortable life. Socially, his mother mingled with the German upper crust. When the Nazi party came to power, with their brown shirts and swastika flags, she dismissed them as "riffraff", and "low class gangsters". Who is this Hitler, she would exclaim. He never completed an education. He is not even German; he is Austrian, and was just a low- class corporal who served in the first World War.

Ever since Hans was young, she instilled in him the hate of the Nazis and what they stood for. His mother, on the other hand, had the vision of foreseeing danger ahead of everybody else. The rapid rise of the para military

Hitler Youth movement, which attracted youngsters from the age of 14, alarmed her. Her son Hans could be under pressure from his peers to join them. In 1933, the campaign against the German Jews started by confiscating their property then putting them in concentration camps. All his family were Christians, there was, therefore, no reason for undue alarm. However, in 1936, Goebbels made a speech calling for the purification of the German race. His mother was proven right in sensing danger. Hans maternal grandfather had married a Jew. Never mind that his paternal grandfather and wife as well as his parents were all Christians. For the Nazi party purists, the family was tainted by one partner three generations back.

His mother wanted him out of the country, before it was too late. When Hans finished his secondary education, his mother had him register at the University of Basel in Switzerland. He was sixteen years old at the time. His mother visited him regularly in Basel, opening a Bank account there in his and her name, and bringing money from Germany for deposit on each visit. His studies in economics were proceeding well, but he was following, with alarm, the developing situation in his home country. Hitler's ambitions seemed to have no bound. There was the annexation of Austria, then Czechoslovakia, the latter move brought Europe to the brink of war. Hans felt an urge to fight, to rid Germany from Hitler and his acolytes. As a German, there was only one way to do so; by joining the French Foreign Legion. The Legion accepted all nationalities, no questions asked. He applied, went for an interview, and was accepted. Recruits in the legion enlist under assumed names and do not need to divulge their past. His enlistment for training was due to start in France on the 4th of September 1939.

On the second of September, one day before Hitler invaded Poland sparking the war, his mother took a train to its terminal station at Badische Bahnhof in Basle. She disembarked, and as usual walked the 100 meters to the border, carrying only her handbag and a small suitcase. At the meshed iron fence, she was met by three German guards. An SS officer looked at her passport, noted the various previous entry stamps to Switzerland and asked her for the purpose of her crossing the border this time. Calmly, she answered that she was going there to pull her son out of his studies in Basel, so that he can return to Germany and fight for the "Fatherland". He waived her through. That was the last time, his mother, saw Germany. When the war broke out the following day, she resigned to living it out in Switzerland. She died following a short illness shortly before the war ended in 1945.

After rigorous military training, Hans was assigned to an infantry regiment with the Legion which was subsequently deployed to Algeria.

In July 1940, the French army capitulated in France, a ceasefire was proclaimed and General Petain was named head of a French government, stationed in Vichy. It became known as the Vichy Government. The authority of this government extended to roughly half of France. The other half was put under direct German rule.

Soon the Vichy Government began to promote accommodation with Germany if not outright cooperation. It accepted various German demands including among others, the deportation of French Jews to concentration camps and the repatriation of French men, to Germany for work in the German war factories. It also, established a militia to trace and liquidate those who promoted resistance to German occupation.

At the same time, and in 1940, a little- known French General, by the name of De Gaulle, escaped to England, established a so- called "Free French Army" to continue the fight against the Germans. French garrisons stationed in the various French colonies had to decide where their loyalty lied, Vichy or the Free French?

The French forces in Algeria went for Vichy. For a year, Hans found himself serving in an army taking orders from German collaborators. That was not what he enlisted for. He resolved to leave his regiment in Algeria and defect to the Free French in London.

Deserting from the Legion was a dangerous adventure. If arrested, he could face up to three years in jail and a major fine. After a year of pondering and planning, he managed to bribe a fisherman to take him together with another Senegalese friend from the Legion, to the British Isles. They left on a weekend when military discipline in the Legion is usually lax. Upon arrival to London, he went to enlist with the Free French, but before he could do so, he was vetted by British intelligence. A German in England during the war, raised suspicions. His service with the Algerian legion, loyal to Vichy, raised more red flags. He could be a spy, no matter how hard, he tried to explain, no one wanted to take the risk of believing his story. He was arrested, and treated as a German prisoner of war. Six months later he was shipped to Canada. When quizzed by fellow prisoners, he would simply say he was captured on the western front, in France. If pressed further on details, he would simply say the subject was too painful and he does not want to talk about it.

As I listened to this story, I felt a strong bond with Hans. When we parted, unconsciously I gave him a big hug, and kept it going a few seconds more than usual. He too pressed me hard to his chest. I must also admit that I am now looking at him in a different light. A handsome good looking young man, a human being who suffered fighting for his beliefs and with whom I would like to keep in touch, lending him any assistance if needed.

Paul closed his mother's diary, putting a bookmark on that page. He too felt a sympathy for Hans after reading his life story. Hans sounded like a fine decent man who went through a lot in his life, to uphold his beliefs. He reached for the bundle of letters removing the elastic band.

Chapter Four

Before proceeding further, Paul paused to gather his thoughts. Apart from his war story, Hans, had a daughter called Julie, who works at a hospital in Cobourg. That was barely an hour and a half drive away. That daughter read his mother's love letters to Hans, and may know more about their relations. He should contact her one day. Before that, however, he should go through the letters he had, and continue reading the diary. He wondered how to proceed. Should he read the letters first, or the diary. He thought it better to go by dates, reading both the diary and the corresponding letters for each date. He started with a May letter.

10 May 1950

Dear Anne,

As you suggested, I am writing to give you my news, and in accordance with your wish, I am also addressing you by your first name. My job as a bellboy working the night shift, suits me fine. I start work at 10 p.m. finish at 6 a.m. We are two at that shift with three others working the two other shifts. While the salary we receive is minimal, tips make all the difference. We hand over our tips to a supervisor, who, after deducting a certain percentage for himself, divides them evenly between the members of our bell boys' group.

I wrote to my former Swiss university got a transcript of the courses I attended there, I took these to the admissions at Sir George Williams, not only was I admitted, but I was given credit for several of the courses passed with success in Switzerland. I was so relieved and happy. This means that I could get my bachelor degree in accounting in about two years from now, rather than in four, if I attend the summer courses as well. The other good news is that I am now on a student visa, so I do not have to worry about a residency permit in Canada at least until I finish my education. I owe all this to you, dear Anne. I am most grateful for your kindness and for your warm feelings when we met in Montreal.

At one time, you asked me why I would not return to Germany and I answered that I had no family to return to. That is only part of the story. Dresden, where we lived, was carpet bombed during the war. For four consecutive days, day and night, waves composed of 200 plus planes in each wave, bombed the city. Our family house must have been destroyed and whatever cousins or friends I had there, probably perished in the raids.

Even if I were able to, I cannot contemplate any visit there at present, as Dresden is now situated in East Germany. This is out of bounds for persons like me. With the passing away of my mother in 1945, I find myself alone in this world. Your friendship means a great deal to me.

yours,
Hans

25 August 1951

Dear Anne,

I passed my exams, both winter and summer sessions with high grades. I hope to graduate by the end of next summer. If I did not write earlier, it is not that you were out of mind. Far from it. I still feel shy opening up and telling you about my achievements, problems and whatever else comes to my mind. I long to seeing you again. May I be so bold as to suggest getting together again, if your time permits perhaps during the next Xmas recess. Please let me know. I will not be offended if this cannot be arranged.

yours,
Hans

Paul **tu**rned his attention to a corresponding entry in his mother's diary.

20 December 1951

Hans arrived in Toronto loaded with Xmas gifts for me and my mother. I met him at the train station three days ago. We went to a restaurant where we sat down for a long chat. When I gently scolded him for spending so

much money on presents, he said he had a stroke of good luck. A famous movie star arrived at the hotel late one night. He is not allowed to divulge the names of hotel guests, so he cannot tell me who it was. Hans carried his two suitcases to his suite. The guest did not have Canadian currency on him for a tip, so he asked Hans to wait. He then pulled out of his brief case a picture of himself, signed it, and gave it to him in lieu of a tip. Hans was able to sell that signed picture for $100.

I gave him whatever news of mine I had. He said that he was doing quite well in his studies, but he wanted to seek my advice on another issue. He met a young girl who came from Winnipeg to Montreal to seek work and to learn French at the same time. Her name was Catherine, but everybody called her Katia. She was a third generation Ukrainian born in Canada. There was a large Ukrainian community in Manitoba Provence. They have their own church and cultural center in Winnipeg. He liked her a great deal; they had been out together twice so far. He was thinking of proposing to her, would it work, with him approaching thirty and she is only 19?

I told him that he should postpone it until he graduates and find a job. Although he did not say it, I guess having a Canadian wife would solve his Canadian residency problem. This he has to do by the time he graduates.

We went home after lunch for tea, where I introduced him to my mother. As usual he was his courteous self and my mother liked him. Divulging his personal situation,

attracts me to him. When we parted, and I came to give him the usual peck on the cheek, he asked me if he can have a hug instead, so sweet of him. We exchanged phone numbers.

20 June 1952

Dear Anne,

As I mentioned on the phone, I wanted so much to have you attend my marriage at the Town Hall. I understand very well the circumstances that prevented you from doing so. At any rate, this was a civil wedding, without much ceremony as I could not afford anything else. Katia and I want to thank you very much for your beautiful wedding gift. It is very thoughtful of you. I have another good news. I found a job!

I start next week as an accountant working for a company in Montreal. Though this is a medium size concern, it remains basically a family run business, where two brothers act both as owners and managers. I am very happy and feel that my future is now settled. I long to see you again and to resume our conversations, but for now I must content with our phone calls.

As ever, yours,
Hans

10 March 1953

Call me Jeff, that is what he said, when I was introduced to Geoffrey Nolan, at a noisy Xmas party. We had since seen each other rather regularly. I wanted to find out

at first, if he was fanatical about pursuing hockey and football results, he was not. He also said that he played golf, had his good and bad days, but had no reason to boast of his exploits at the game. This put him in a better standing in my estimation. He worked for an insurance company, and he enlightened me a bit about the intricacies of the insurance business, a subject I was faintly interested in, though I did not show it. Two weeks ago, he proposed. I told my mother, who said that if he was a steady person with a good job, then that is all that mattered, adding that at 31 years old, I should not be too demanding. I like Jeff, he is a nice person, I am not sure I am in love with him though. To think that I would lose sleep, if I did not see him daily would be a great exaggeration. Last week, I gave him my consent with two conditions. First, I want to retain my Hamilton family name. Second, I want to wait a while before having children as this may entail giving up work. I was not ready to do that in the immediate future. He readily agreed, and so we are engaged. He suggested that we get married next September and go to Myrtle Beach in North Carolina for our honeymoon. I welcomed the idea.

Hans called saying he would like to bring Katia to Toronto to meet me, and proposed next weekend.

22 April 1954

Hans showed up alone at the train station. He gave me a red rose. I gave him a kiss on the cheek, in return. He apologized profusely saying that at the last minute,

Katia had a headache and could not make it. He added sarcastically, that she usually has headaches on Wednesdays and Saturdays. I sensed that something was wrong in their marriage, and gently quizzed him about it.

He said, it was probably all his fault, that things do not seem to be working out as he would have liked. This may be due to his German straight lace upbringing, and his military disciplinary training. He often made a fuss if things were not in order. Katia was a nice simple girl, but he gets upset if he finds coffee cups lying around, or dirty dishes kept for hours in the sink. At times, he shows his unhappiness by shouting with a loud voice. He also gets angry, if he came for lunch, as he sometimes does, and finds her still in her nightgown watching TV soap operas. It irritates him as well, that Katia thinks that making up and being presentable is something to be done only if she was going out.

This tendency for abiding by discipline, and playing by the rules, was also affecting him at work, he added. A few months after starting to work, he noticed a false entry in the books. One of the owners took a pleasure trip with his wife and charged that expense to the company. It was entered as a business trip taken with an assistant. He wanted to correct that entry, when he was called over by his superior.

– Listen, son. You are new here. Let me tell you a story. Three accountants like yourself, applied for a job. During the interview, all three were asked the same question:

What is one plus one? The first said it was two. The second hesitated then said: "Under certain conditions, the answer is two." The third who was hired on the spot, gave the correct answer "How much do you want it to be?"

In this company, his superior added, we were hired and we work hard with one objective in mind; to maximize the profits for the owners. The marketing people do it by increasing sales, the production people by cutting production costs, and we as accountants, our contribution is to reduce the amount of taxes, the owners must pay, provided of course, that we do not get caught by other accountants in the Tax Department.

Hans told me that conversation affected him deeply. He was expected to twist accounting rules to suit the owners. This ran against his grain. He began to question himself. Was he brought up to live in Eutopia where everything was well organized and everybody abided by the rules? Or, should he get used to real life, with all its shortcomings and adopt a laissez-faire attitude?

I could sense the dilemma, he faced, for like many others, I sometimes, faced similar situations. I told him, though I did not entirely believe it, that this had nothing to do with his upbringing, that we all, at one time or another, face similar issues. He just needed to relax, ignore all these imperfections that invariably breed unhappiness. He thanked me saying that I was the only person in the world, who gave him comfort. We parted with a big hug.

George Kanawaty

17 September 1955

My Dear Anne,

My warmest congratulations on your wedding. Although I never met Jeff, I am sure that he is a fine man who will make you very happy. I say so, because I know that you are not a person who awards her affection lightly or to the non-deserving. I wish you both all the happiness in the world.

I will be shortly changing jobs for the better. I applied to the seven largest accounting firms in the world, the so-called the big seven. I was interviewed by two of them and just received and accepted an offer from Ernst &Young. The salary, working hours and probably the work ethics are much better. I think I will also learn more by working at such a well-renown and large firm with branches worldwide.

I wish I can kiss the bride. I hope we can continue to be in touch. A big hug.

Yours as always,
Hans

10 October 1958

My Dear Anne,

Just a brief note to tell you that we have a baby girl. I wanted so much to call her Anne, but Katia insisted on naming her Juliette, so that later in life she can find her Romeo, or so she said. She had become infatuated with the story of Romeo and

Juliette after watching the play on TV. Little Julie is such a beautiful baby, I always rush to be with her as soon as I come home from work. I feel so happy discovering and doing mundane things, like changing her diapers, feeding her, or carrying her to bed. I wish you were here to share this feeling with me. Miss you.

Yours as always,
Hans

Paul folded the diary, put aside the letters, and started looking, once more, at the pictures in the accompanying small brown envelope. When he first discovered that his mother was fond of someone other than his father, he was inclined to dislike him. Now that he has read the diary and Hans's letters, he had the opposite feeling. Hans was a decent amiable man, and if he made his mother happy, that should make him happy too. He looked more attentively, at the pictures; there was Hans in his twenties at his college graduation, then with his mother by the lake in Toronto, then in his thirties, with a baby, then there was a picture of him with his mother by the Eiffel tower in Paris. Other pictures showed them together in other places, he did not recognize. Paul was full of emotions. How did this story unfold?

Chapter Five

2 November 1958

Hans last letter describing his affection towards his newly born baby, got me thinking. Maybe it was time I too, got my own baby. I am at a respectable age to be a mother. A baby could fill up a void in my life. Jeff is a very nice person who caters to my material needs, without a fuss. He also helps with the shopping and whenever I need him at home. However, there is something wanting in him. I failed to get him interested in classical concerts, literature, history, world affairs and the list goes on.

He is often away on business. We seem to have run out of subjects to talk about. Contrast this with Hans, when I think about it. Whenever Hans and I meet or talk on the phone, time seems to run out, before we finish exchanging views on various cultural, historical, or current affairs. I often feel stimulated to think more of issues that I had lightly dismissed or overlooked after talking to him.

I wonder what pregnancy will be like, but for now I am determined to bring a baby of mine to life.

14 November 1960

I cannot help wanting to continuously hold my baby in my arms. I am determined to breast feed him. We called him Paul in honor of Jeff's father. In return, Jeff agreed, to him having the Hamilton family name. It was a difficult pregnancy and an equally difficult delivery. I went through a cesarian operation and the doctor cautioned me about getting pregnant again. I want to be a fulltime mother so I resigned my job. I proudly showed Paul to my mother. She was so happy, holding him in her arms. Jeff too is also very happy being a father.

I heard from Hans. He got what he wanted. A transfer to his company's Paris Branch. He told me on the phone, that his fluency in French, his university education in both Switzerland and Canada, helped as well as his German nationality. That nationality, allows him to work in France and in any other European country, without a work permit. He, of course, will also keep his Canadian citizenship. He leaves to Paris early next January. He wants to come to Toronto to say goodbye. Will be very happy to see him again, and sorry to see him go.

12 December 1960

This was a memorable day. Let me start from the beginning. I left little Paul with mother, reserved at a

Lebanese restaurant in Toronto where Hans and I, could meet for a nice chat and a good meal. He brought me a red rose and a stuffed little toy for Paul. We kissed on the cheek in what he often referred to as "a brother to sister kiss". We sat down and I asked him, how it felt getting anew a German nationality. He said, he has been living in Canada now for over seventeen years, thanks to me, who helped me get his first job and settle in this country. A country, he loves. He was both grateful and proud that he was accepted and awarded a Canadian citizenship. However, he has not been successful in breaking altogether, the umbilical cord that tied him emotionally to his country of origin. He continues to follow developments there, almost daily. It disturbed him to see the division of Germany in East and West. The devastation that took place in the country after the war was horrendous, to say the least, but he also discovered that his country suffered another blow that is hardly ever mentioned. A blow directed at its manufacturing base. His company hires part time consultants, from time to time, to perform specific jobs, such as speakers at conferences that they organize.

One of those consultants, is a Professor at the University of Illinois, who invited him on several occasions to bring his wife and spend a weekend with them. He told him that if he came for a visit, he will have a surprise for him. One day, he made it to Champaign Urbana, home of the University of Illinois, where that professor lived. The surprise in question consisted of him being taken by the professor to visit the university library.

— You are of a German origin, are you not? Perhaps, then, you will be interested in looking at these, said the professor, pointing to a shelf stacked with tens of leather- bound volumes. Each volume, contained tens of pamphlets.

The professor then picked a volume, leafed through the pamphlets inside until he found what he was looking for and showed it to him. The title was "The Bayer Company Aspirin Plant." Hans recalled that in the 1930's the composition and manufacturing of Bayer Aspirin was Bayer's closely guarded secret. Nobody, at the time, knew the composition of Aspirin, nor how it was made. That pamphlet exposed everything. It consisted of an interview with the company management, run by the Office of Strategic services (OSS) a precursor to the CIA, and which was conducted immediately after the war. It described the composition of Aspirin, its manufacturing process, together with a diagram showing the production flow, the output, the number of workers involved and their working hours.

In other words, the whole supposedly confidential information, of making aspirin was now mass produced in pamphlets put on the market for sale, by that intelligence agency, at 25 US cents each.

The same was done for almost every manufacturing concern in the country. Hans picked up another pamphlet. It described a factory making submarine torpedoes. It described the factory as 20% destroyed, the workers all females working two 12 hours shifts. It made him wonder whether these were forced labor or German women motivated by war propaganda. He felt so sorry for those workers. On another shelf, nearby, in the library lay another set of volumes, though much less in number. They were like the ones he has just seen, but were produced by British intelligence.

In short, in addition to all the physical destruction done to the country during the war, the intellectual property of German industry was also dismantled, and put on sale for a very cheap price.

Despite all that, Germany, at least West Germany, from what he hears, seems to have overcome reconstruction and development hurdles and was even prospering. He had an urge to want to visit his home country again, even if he could not go to Dresden, which was now in East Germany. He was hoping to do so, from his new post in Paris.

I asked Hans, if he was excited at the prospect of going to live in Paris. He said he knows a lot about Paris, but does not know the city, as he had never visited it. Can you imagine, he told me, Paris has at least, ten must see, museums and a multitude of smaller ones. It has seven opera houses, three major orchestras and so on. He longed to immerse himself in this culture and to bring up little Julie to appreciate it as well. As soon as she grows up a little, he wants to take her to visit museums, watch ballet and listen to concerts.

My dear Anne, he added, if only you too, can join me, my happiness would have no bound. I keep wanting to forget that you are married and now a mother. Will you come one day, for a visit and bring Paul with you.

Once more, I stretched my hand and pressed his. Deep inside, I longed to explore Paris with him. I added, alas, that was not possible, but promised to keep in touch, either in writing or by phoning.

When it was time to part, he said, you know our lips have never met and proceeded to want to kiss me. I longed for that kiss and wanted it, but found myself putting my hand across his lips, preventing this to happen. I told him while in his arms for a long hug, that we should restrain whatever feelings we have, since we are both married. So far, we have not done anything that obliges us to lie about, to Katia and Jeff, and we need to keep it that way. When he left, I wondered if I will ever see him again, I could feel my misty eyes as I waived him goodbye. Were we in love with each other? Was there a phrase that describes a love that is deeply felt but never declared?

2 February 1962

Just returned from my mother's funeral. Her departure and Paul's arrival, made me think of the essence of life. Does it have to be that one person must exit to make room for a new arrival? I will miss my mother greatly. Whatever she lacked in education, she made up for it by reading. She subscribed to a national daily, the Toronto

Globe and Mail, to the National Geographic magazine, and occasionally she bought books dealing with certain topics that interested her. She had her close circle of friends, all with a Mediterranean ethnic background. Two women were Lebanese, one was Greek and two were Italian. They often met for coffee and a chat, at each other's homes, where homemade cookies or cake was served, I will certainly miss the Lebanese food she occasionally prepared. Although she taught me how to make some dishes, I will never match her flair in cooking. No matter how I tried to have the ingredients she used, measured correctly so that I can record this or that recipe on paper, she often added a bunch of something here and there to bring it to the taste she wanted. I call that flair; it was difficult for me to measure and record these little extras. Rest in Peace Mom.

Hans phoned. I was so eager to hear his voice. He found an apartment in Paris, a walking distance from a subway station. He also found a kindergarten for Julie. He said it will take time for Katia to get used to living there. He is happy at work. He found out that the Paris Ernst & Young is sometimes called on to do work in former French colonies in Africa and the Far East. He will keep me posted. He said he misses me terribly. I surprised myself by telling him "Me too"! From now on, I am resolved not to suppress my feelings anymore. I think of him almost daily, wondering what was he doing, recalling every sentence or gesture that hid a loving intent.

I have dated many men since my teenager years, sometimes convincing myself to be in love, only to have such relations wither within weeks or months. In all these cases, I never experienced such deep feelings as I feel now. Feelings that took time to mature and grow roots. I am in love with him, of that I am certain.

8 September 1962

Dearest Anne,

Every time I hear your voice on the phone, it gives me such pleasure and sadness at the same time. I am sad that we cannot say to each other what we want to say face to face. Invariably after I hang up, I remember things that I forgot to mention, or that came to my mind too late for me to say.

My news this time is not all good. Katia, has been diagnosed here with breast cancer. For months, she had felt a lump in her breast, but with her laissez faire attitude, she thought it would disappear and kept putting off seeing a doctor. It was not easy to get an appointment with a gynecologist here, and it took a long time for her to get a mammography at a hospital as well. Finally, when she got to see the doctor for the results, he told her that she had an advanced case of breast cancer and that a lengthy treatment would be needed. She told me she did not trust the French doctors nor their medical system. She wanted to be treated in Canada. I finally agreed with her decision to return to Winnipeg for medical treatment where she would be close to her family. She will take little Julie with her. I dearly miss them specially Julie. Katia phoned me from Winnipeg to tell me that she started the chemo therapy which made her sick, the doctors there sound hopeful but non-comital at the same time. I pray for her recovery and safe return with Julie. I call Julie every evening to wish her a goodnight.

Will write or phone again once I have more news.

With all my love as always.

Hans

16 May 1963

Anne, my dearest,

As I mentioned on the phone, I keep praying that Katia will pull through. I spoke to the treating doctor again today. He said that the chances of her recovery are fifty-fifty as he put it, given that the cancer has now spread to another organ. They will keep doing their best. If there is life, there is hope, he told me.

At work, I had lunch with a colleague yesterday. He just returned from an auditing job of a public corporation in a North African country, that I cannot name. It concerned a state-owned publishing company. A few years back all publishing activities in that country were nationalized and put under one entity. That meant that all newspapers, magazines, books and so on were now put under this one, Government-owned and run, concern. A constant critic of the Government, a parliamentarian and ex-minister was put in charge of that now public company. He was given a good renumeration as a result, which was also meant to silence him. However, three years later and after a new Prime Minister was appointed, he kept his open criticism of what he saw as nepotism and corruption at higher levels in the government. Worse, he had at his disposal, the tools to publicize his thoughts. The call to Ernst & Young for an audit of that company by the government, was intended, my colleague surmised, to find an excuse to silence this manager by putting him in jail for a long time. My colleague was put under pressure to produce a condemning report. He did not, he produced a factual one.

In my early career as an accountant, I was unhappy, when accounting practices were tailored to suit certain interests. Now I see that it can be used as well, as a political tool to punish opponents.

I hope I am not boring you with this my dear Anne. If I mentioned it, it is because my turn has come to go on an international assignment. It is an assignment in Cambodia, for an audit requested by the Michelin company concerning its operations there. Michelin owns a large rubber plantation in Cambodia, and apart from auditing, I am to propose improvements, if any, of their bookkeeping and accounting practices. I will be leaving next October, following the end of the rainy season there. I am excited, as I have never been to that part of the world. Will write you from there, as I am told phoning would be difficult. I have also been told that personal mail delivery in the country does not exist, one goes to the Post office to collect his or her mail. Foreign mail service is also slow, so responding to my mail is not advisable. My assignment could take two to three months.

Miss you terribly, send you all my love as always,

Hans

Chapter Six

Pnom Penh, 12 November 1963

Dearest Anne,

Here I am in Cambodia. I arrived over a month ago, was met at the airport by a Michelin company representative, who drove me to the hotel Royale, where I am staying. The hotel boasts the only swimming pool in the country. It is surrounded by a well-kept lawn, flowers, and some tropical trees. Hardly anybody goes there during the daytime, as the temperature often tops the 44 degrees Celsius, with close to 75% humidity in the dry season, and close to 100% in the rainy season. My room is comfortable, and the air conditioning unit, which runs continuously, manages to bring the room temperature down, to around 26 degrees. People flock to have drinks around the pool, only in the late evening when it is cooler. The hotel personnel, then, place smoking green coils around the tables to chase the mosquitos away, particularly since a high percentage of these are malaria bearing. The food at the hotel is good but expensive, which is not surprising as Cambodia seems to import everything and export mainly two commodities; rice and natural rubber from the Michelin plantation.

I plan to use, this opportunity, to expand my knowledge of the country and not to act solely as an outsider, interested only in accounting books and procedures. I have been lucky in that an employee of the company was attached to me during my mission. Because of your interest in foreign cultures, I thought I would write, to share my experience here, with you.

The capital of Cambodia, a country with close to six million population, is Pnom Penh. This city, a vestige of French colonial past, is relatively clean. Many of its streets are lined with bougainvillea and tamarind trees. Near the Presidential palace, there are small manicured gardens, and there are benches for those who wish to sit and watch boats, navigating the Mekong River in front. The streets are all one lane each way, with one exception, a 200 meters boulevard, with two lanes each way leading to an ancient temple, called the Pnom, which serves as a national heroic symbol, tomb of the unknown soldier, as well as a symbol for various commemorations. A huge building in the city houses the central market, where one can buy wonderful tropical fruits, vegetables, fish and seafood, meat, mainly pork and chicken. No dairy products, and beef is rare. Interesting to note that all the vendors are women. At the same market, one can also buy dry goods such as sandals and clothes.

The traffic in the city is busy with scooters, and hundreds of "pousse-pousse" (push-push), also known as "Cyclos" clogging the streets, as well as tri-cycle motorized small taxis. The cyclos, consist of a tri-cycle, at which you sit on a chair with a canopy shading your head from sunshine or rain, with a person seated behind you who cycles you around. No dialogue with him is needed. If you point to the right, it means turn right, and the same for the left, if you say nothing, he cycles you straight ahead; and if you waive your hand a couple of time pointing to the pavement, it means let me down here. You then pay the standard fare, five Riyals or less usually for the nationals and ten for the foreigners. I am happy to tell you that I used these cyclos a few times.

The ruler of the country is the very popular Prince Norodom Sihanouk, who also goes by the titles of "Monsignor, Chef d'état and protector of Buddhism". The Americans here call him "Snookie", something I do not condone. His popularity is due to his direct and frequent communication with his people. He often comes on the radio to recount his thoughts and ideas, even if these were personal, like his impending visit to France for a cure to shed some weight. News of his family and jokes are interspersed with his views on international affairs, in speeches, or radio talks, that can last a couple of hours each. The prince also often descends unannounced by a helicopter, on poor villages to distribute cloth material produced by one of his four public owned companies. In addition, I was told, he also holds once a year, a political rally lasting three to four days at the capital's stadium, at which any person can raise any question to any of his ministers in attendance. This event is broadcast live on the radio. Television does not exist here.

Work-wise, I was driven to the Michelin rubber plantations two days after my arrival, spent three days there visiting, examining the books interviewing managers and raising questions. The nicely kept plantation is surrounded by tropical forests and the windy road leading there, was carved through that forest. On the way back, my colleague guide, suggested we stop by the little town of Kampot, the country's prominent producer of Black pepper, a product of international reputation. I bought a couple of kilos, one for you, my dearest, as a souvenir of this trip.

After my return to Pnom Penh, my colleague informed me that the offices would be closed for the next three days as it was the water festival, a national holiday. When I asked him what I could do during this time, he suggested that I visit the famous Angkor Wat. I am so glad I did. I reached it by taking a plane to Siam Riep then a taxi to the site. A tourist guide I hired, explained that historical complex to me. There were several Angkor sites to visit of which Angkor wat is the most visited, but there was also Angkor Tom and others. These temples and palaces were erected around the twelve century when Cambodia, a major power, had flexed its muscles occupying parts of present-day Vietnam and Thailand, these various Angkors, covered tens of square kilometers. Then in the fourteenth century, the Thais invaded the country and ransacked the sites, which were then deserted and forgotten. Gradually, tropical vegetation and forests threw their mantle over the whole area. The existence of Angkor became a tale shrouded in mystery. It was only in the 1920's that a French expedition rediscovered the site. Since then, a monumental task was taken to free these temples from creeping roots of trees and vegetation. How I wish you were here with me to contemplate the history of those who lived there, centuries ago and to admire these magnificent monuments.

After three more weeks of work, I finished my assignment. I proposed a revamping of the accounting system used, proposed a new more proficient one and suggested my return in six months, to review its application. My proposals were entertained favorably at the local level, with a final report to be presented to the Michelin headquarters in Paris, later.

I board the Air France plane this coming Sunday back to Paris. This is a flight that leaves Paris to Hong Kong and stops in Pnom Penh once a week on the Saturday, bringing with it cargo, mail but also the much-awaited journal "Le Monde", a lifeline to foreigners, anxious for international and French news. On its way back, from Hong Kong, that flight makes another stop in Pnom Penh, where I will board. I am anxious to get Katia and Julie's news and will phone you, my dearest, from Paris on arrival.

I have no idea if this letter will reach you before my call, but I will take my chances and mail it just the same. I missed you terribly on this trip particularly during the visit to Angkor.

Yours as ever,
Hans

Bangkok, 27 March 1964

My dearest Anne,

My Xmas vacation spent in Winnipeg, was not a merry one. I saw the deterioration in Katia's health, and my earlier optimism, has been replaced by a sense of resignation, especially after a discussion with the oncology doctor. I tried my best to cheer her up, but I was sad. Spent all my days, with her at the hospital, with a few exceptions when I took Julie out shopping, to the skating rink, or to McDonalds. We opened our Xmas presents by Katia's bedside at the hospital.

I flew back to Paris right after the new year and immersed myself in work. That included scheduling my return trip to Cambodia for this March. My plan was to arrive to Pnom Penh, on Saturday the 14th, for a week.

As you probably know, the Americans started bombing Vietnam in early March. At my company we were not unduly alarmed. Cambodia was another country, declared neutral in the conflict by Sihanouk. Besides, Ernst & Young had to honor its contract with Michelin. As a result, I arrived Pnom Penh as planned. A few days of meetings and records examinations convinced me that my proposals were implemented, with minor problems that were soon ironed out. My return flight to Paris was confirmed for Sunday, the 22nd.

On the 19th. of March, I got the news, that the US air force in pursuing the Vietcong trail which at times passed through Cambodian territory, bombed Chantrea village, six kilometers into Cambodian territory. That raid resulted in 17 villagers killed and 13 injured. The reaction of Sihanouk was swift. He summoned the US and British ambassadors, flew with them in a helicopter to the bombed- out village to show them the damage done, condemned that unwarranted attack on his country, and asked for a compensation for the victims. Later that day, he made a fiery speech broadcast on the radio lamenting the attack by "the imperialists" on his peaceful country and on poor villagers. He then called for the boycott of the "Anglo-Saxons". The following morning, I received a phone call from the local Michelin colleague, advising me to stay put at the hotel and not to leave it until further notice. That day, the mob, egged on by a loudspeaker, organized by a left-leaning Minister, stormed the British council setting it on fire, attacked the British Embassy, then went on to attack the US Embassy, whereby the marines defending the building opened fire.

A stalemate existed around that embassy. A day later, another phone call informed me that it was not possible or safe, for them to drive me to the airport, some 15 kilometers away, as the unruly mob were roaming and blocking several streets. My Air France flight was cancelled. I had to wait and give the Michelin office here, more time to make alternative arrangements. It was only on the Friday 27th. that it became safe, for the office here, to drive me to the airport where I boarded a flight to Bangkok. The respite came after another speech by Sihanouk, when he then accused the communists of exploiting the situation, whereby the crowds stopped their harassment of the "Anglo-Saxons".

I Leave tomorrow to Paris. I will always remember that week in Pnom Penh. At the hotel, where I and other foreigners were holed up, we lived in fear that the mob may attack us. We were hanging on whatever news and rumors we could get, hour by hour. Glad I made it to safety. I do hope that this once peaceful country and its people do not become the causality of another war.

I regret that I do not have more cheerful news to give you currently. A big hug.

as ever yours,
Hans

Winnipeg 10 May 1964

Dearest Anne,

With a heavy heart. I am sad to inform you that Katia passed away a week ago. I flew to Winnipeg and spent the last two days of her life with her. I saw to her funeral at the Ukrainian church here, and to her burial at her family's plot. I will be spending some more time here to sort things out and am planning on taking Julie with me back to Paris. We fly to Paris, via Toronto. We arrive to Toronto Pearson airport from Winnipeg at 4:30 p.m. by West Jet, on the Thursday ten days from now, changing to Air France two and a half hours later. If there is any chance of your being able to meet us at Toronto airport, that would induce a ray of sunshine in what has been a sad and a dark chapter in my life. If you cannot make it, that would be totally understandable.

Yours,
Hans

Paul set aside that letter from Hans, which was the last but one in the bundle. The last was written almost forty years later, announcing Hans's hospitalization, prior to his death. His mother and Hans must have continued their contacts by phone instead of writing, he figured. He also noticed, that there were no more entries in his mother's diary. What went on during these missing years. Could Julie, now at Cobourg shed more light on that, he wondered.

Chapter Seven

It was a sunny, but a cool day, when Anne Hamilton drove that Thursday 21 May 1964 to Toronto's Pearson airport. On arrival, she headed to the national arrival gate, waiting for Winnipeg passengers. For a few days now, she had been struggling with her own contradictory feelings. Deep inside, she longed to take Hans in her arms, kiss him, and tell him that she loved him. But then, how could she even contemplate such a move with a person who had just lost his wife. She needs to subdue her feelings, at least for now. She needs also to remember, that she is already married to a good man, who loved her in his own way. She cannot possibly sideline him and her son, for a romance in the making.

When Hans and little Julie, showed up, she rushed to them, gave Hans the tightest hug she could, and brushed her lips against his in a brief passing kiss, and hugged little Julie. Hans told his little girl:

— Meet aunty Anne.

—   Hans. I am so sorry for your losing Katia. My deep
     sympathies.

He acknowledged her condolences with a nod. They had
over an hour of spare time to kill, before heading to the Air
France boarding gate. They walked leisurely before finding
a bench to sit. Julie was given permission to wonder about,
if she did not stray far.

Their few minutes of silence was broken by Anne.

—   What plans do you have for Julie, when you get to
     Paris?
—   I will enroll her in the international school, where
     she could still get a grounding in English, apart
     from French. The graduation certificate obtained
     from that school is recognized in Europe, as well as
     in the US and Canada, which would enable her to
     enroll into various universities there, that is, if she
     wished to pursue her studies.

I also plan to gradually introduce her to the various cultural
events that Paris offers.

—   I hope you are coping with the loss of Katia, Hans.
     It is not easy, I know.
—   She leaves a void in my life, that is for sure. What
     was painful, was to see her wither gradually, with
     me being helpless, unable to do anything about it. I
     suppose I will get over it, with time. At present, I feel
     alone. You are the only close friend that I have left.

She held his hand and pressed it.

- — And I feel very close to you too Hans.
- — Please Anne, let us not allow the physical distance between you in Toronto and me in Paris, separate us. I need you now more than ever. I promise not to be crying on your shoulder, I just want to feel that you are there for me. I want to be assured occasionally, that I am still in your thoughts, and that you continue to hold some affection for me.
- — You will always have my affection.
- — Can we keep in touch by phone. Would you allow me to call you, weekly or better twice a week.
- — By all means. I would love to hear from you, as often as you like. Twice a week would be great.
- — That makes me very happy. He paused.
- — I must confess. I think of you often, and daily.

Anne looked at him. The look in her eyes bore more than words could say. He

He put his arm around her shoulder, brought her closer to him.

- — I am and have been in love with you all my life Anne. I know I do not have the right to say that, but I cannot help it.

Anne's response was to press her lips against his, in a long often dreamt of kiss, and to whisper:

- — I love you too my Hans.

Hans let off a smile adding;

> – Here we are having our first kiss, and our first love
> declaration, in one of the most unromantic places
> on earth, a busy airport hall. Shortly thereafter,
> they started their way to the Air France gate. Anne
> waived them goodbye, sending a kiss floating in the
> air to both Hans and little Julie.

When Anne drove back home, she felt twenty years younger.
Happy, like a teenager who is about to start a new chapter in
her life. On arrival home, she picked up four years old Paul,
hugged and kissed him. Hans and Paul, for sure, were the
two most beloved persons in her life.

At night, and although she shared the same bed with Jeff,
her thoughts were elsewhere. Will the day ever come, when
it would be Hans instead, who would be lying beside her.

For hours, Anne, lay wide awake, pondering the prospects
of her new, so far, plutonic love. She day dreamt of all
sorts of future encounters and adventures, of meetings in
faraway places, of bent up emotions let loose, and of untold
enjoyment and happiness. It was only around four in the
morning, that she finally fell into a deep sleep, without
feeling Jeff getting out of bed for work.

Later that same morning, she received her first call from
Paris. She and Hans used terms of endearment for the first
time. He filled her in, on his latest news, his flight, Julie's
reaction returning home after almost a couple of years of
absence and their plans for the coming weekend. He was

to phone again three days later, the coming Monday to be precise.

The phone calls now settled to a pattern, he phoned every Monday and Thursday. To keep this relation confidential, it was Hans who placed the calls. If need be, she could call him, particularly in an emergency. She did so on occasions, calling him from a public phone one time, to say that she could not wait three more days to hear his voice. On another occasion, she phoned to complain that she had a bad dream. She dreamt that he was having an affair with another woman.

Anne's phone conversation, consisted of relaying to him her daily shores, Paul's scholastic records, the usual dose of political issues in Canada, and the US., and thoughts about international affairs. These were interspersed by expressions of love and sadness at being so far apart.

A red rose was delivered to her on the 21st. of May, no card was attached. She knew it was the commemoration of their love declaration at the airport. This became a yearly event. It always awoke in her the ardent desire for him, and invited the inevitable comparison with her current life with her husband, Jeff.

Come to think of it, she, and Jeff, also used words of endearment. They addressed each other often as "darling". But this word has been used constantly, for so many years, that it wore out its glamor, bordering on the irrelevance.

Hearing from Hans about the various cultural events to which he was taking his little girl in Paris, only exacerbated her feeling of an arid cultural life with Jeff. Did she marry the wrong man? Surely, Jeff shared with her mostly everything; his career worries and setbacks and their financial situation. They had a limited circle of friends, and they occasionally entertained and were entertained in return. But time was passing by, and she was not getting younger. She was missing out on the true profound love that Hans can amply provide.

In another phone call, Hans told her that he took Julie on his 1965 summer leave to the south of France. They enjoyed their time by the beach in Cannes, and for the following summer, he was planning on driving with her to visit a few cities in Germany. He was thinking of spending the following vacation of the summer of 1967 up north in Scandinavian countries, either driving by car or taking a cruise. He told her as he often did, how he longed to have her share these trips. He knew that would not be possible, but if she could find a way to make it happen, that would put him in seventh heaven.

Anne had only gone once before, to Europe, specifically to the UK. That was with a group of teenagers, when they just finished high school. It was lots of fun. They visited points of interest in the London greater area, like Windsor Castle, the Tower of London, ST. Paul cathedral, but mostly enjoyed themselves going to pubs and to dancing events. From what Hans has been telling her, there was so much to see and enjoy in continental Europe. To do so, in the company of the man she loves would be heaven on earth. She needs to find a way without hurting Jeff's feelings or compromising her marriage. How? She does not know, but she will keep thinking of a way to make it happen.

A year passed, before Jeff told her that all was not well with him. For a couple of months, he has been having a problem passing urine. It took a month before he could see his general doctor, and two more before an appointment with a urologist could be arranged. A referral was made for a biopsy test at a hospital before the urologist gave them the diagnosis. He had a prostate cancer. The doctor, did not show an undue alarm, adding that prostate cancer was common for men above a certain age. He was reassuring, saying, you do not usually die from prostate cancer, you die with it. The implication was, that it is a long- lasting disease. The main concern was to prevent the cancer spreading to the bones or to other parts such as the colon. He will have him follow a treatment and will check things out six months later.

Six months passed. Upon further tests, the doctor told them that the treatment was not producing the results he was hoping for. Surgery was therefore recommended. Before taking that step, however, there was one thing to consider. A surgery like that, followed by radiation, will impair Jeff's sexual drive. They were to think about it and let him know. At any rate, it will take a while to find a spot in the busy operating rooms schedule.

Anne urged Jeff to go ahead with the operation. It made no sense to her, doing nothing, but suffering, without even a cure in perspective. At any rate, their sexual encounters had been, so far in between, that it did not matter much, if it dwindled to nothing. After some hesitation, Jeff reluctantly agreed. The prostate cancer operation was carried out early in 1970. A radiation treatment followed. While the treatment may be described as moderately successful, its side effects left Jeff weak, walking slower than usual, and suffering from sleep deprivation.

He took the decision to quit work, he was slightly over sixty years old, and deserved to retire. Anne always drove him for treatment, and tried to keep up his morale.

When she relayed this situation to Hans, he told her that instead of spending his vacation in northern Europe, he will come to Canada to be near her. In the summer of 1971, Hans met her in Toronto. He flew with Julie to Winnipeg, left her there with his in- laws for a week before heading to Toronto for a week.

They met every day for a couple of hours, happy to be in each other's company and arms. It was all plutonic, lovely to remember, but not enough to satisfy the desire they felt for each other. If only she could come to Paris when they can spend days together, not hours, he told her. He added that the whole of France goes on vacation every year, after the 14th of July, the national day. Half the Paris population desert the city to go on vacations either in France itself, or to other countries. Many businesses close for the summer vacation, until the "rentrer" or the return, that is at the beginning of September. If it can be arranged, that summer period would be an ideal time for them to be together, as he too will be on an extended leave. He knows, however, that this was a dream, that cannot become real.

Anne kept thinking about this possibility. She loved the idea, but how can she leave her husband and child. She was devoted to them, but should this devotion deprive her from a couple of weeks of sheer happiness in the company of Hans in another country. She was already in her late forties, and time was passing by quicker than she would have liked. She deserved a break from the usual routine. She must find a way.

The idea came to her through the junk mail left in their mailbox almost daily. It was an advertisement for organized tours to various parts of Europe including France.

Over dinner, she casually told her husband:

- I saw an advertisement for a guided tour to France in the junk mail today. I have always wanted to see France, before it is too late. It would have been lovely if we could go together, this coming summer, but I realize that this may be too much for you.
- Yes. I am afraid, I cannot make it, but why don't you go?
- I cannot leave you alone with Paul.
- Nonsense. I am not handicapped, I just tire quickly, and if I need to see a doctor or go for a treatment, I can always call a taxi. You have done a lot for me, my dear, you need a break. How long will this tour last?

- there are options, the most attractive is the two
  weeks option.
- well then, I am not going to go to pieces in two
  weeks. Go for it.
- Are you sure?
- Absolutely.

There it was. Jeff made the decision for her. Anne went to see
the travel agent the following day. She was interested in "the
France" tour. She would like to book the one starting the
10th of August and lasting two weeks. As indicated, the tour
starts in Paris, for three days followed by visits to Bretagne,
Normandy (to visit Omaha Beach, scene of the second world
war landing), and then a tour of two chateaus in the Loire
region, before heading back to Paris for the return flight.

Anne told the travel agent that she had one query though.
She had relatives in Paris, who may want to take her out for
family gatherings or for trips of their own. She was not sure
this will happen, but in such an eventuality, could she split
from the group on arrival to Paris and rejoin them for the
return trip. She was given an assurance that there would be
no problem in that respect. She then booked the tour after
ascertaining that the tour director would be alerted to such
an eventuality.

This being settled, Anne immediately called Hans.

- Guess what my darling ! I have a surprise for you. I
  will be coming to Paris next August for two weeks.
- I cannot believe it !! will you be alone?

– Only if you want me to be, in which case, I will. Totally alone.

– Do not tell me I am dreaming again. Where will you be staying? Of course, you can stay with me, but if you feel more comfortable, I can book a hotel room for you.

– I want to be with you, but what about Julie?

– She will be in Montreal at that time.

– Montreal ? why what happened?

– Julie and I have been discussing her future over the last several months. She made up her mind. She wants to go for nursing. This career interests her a great deal. She also wants to pursue her studies at McGill university in Montreal, because of the prevailing French culture in that city, to which she can relate, having spent ten years here. Admission to that prestigious university is not that easy. I also worried about her sudden exposure to the Canadian way of life, if I left it too late. She and I have been making various enquiries. We thought it would be better if she got her pre-university education at a CEGEP in Quebec. This is the equivalent of the last two years of high school in other provinces and countries. She applied to a CEGEP in Montreal and was accepted. She is now 14 years old. I was planning on flying with her to Montreal, finding her a place to live, may be with a family. I then trust that she will make it for this three to four years Bachelor degree in nursing, depending on whether she wants to take summer classes. I retain some

contacts from my previous work in Montreal, which
will be helpful in finding her a suitable place to stay.
– Sorry that I will miss her. Will you be back for 11
August? That is when my plane will land ? Do you
accept me as a guest at your place?
– A guest ? Never. I will only accept you as a lover. I
am overcome with joy, my love.

Yes. I will be back by then.

When Anne hung up, she too was overjoyed, but there was
a sense of doubt that crept into her thinking. They had not
seen each other for two years. Was she still attractive to him
at 48 years. She looked at the mirror. There was only a faint
wrinkle under her eyes, nothing on the neck, and no sign of
any grey strand in her otherwise black hair. What about her
body, which he is likely to see for the first time?

When she got ready for a shower, she examined it in the
mirror. It was no longer in the shape it was, when she
was twenty or thirty years younger. She could see a small
protruding stomach, breasts that lost their firmness and a
shade of cellulite about her thighs. Would that put him off?

After a stop in Montreal, the Air Canada flight from Toronto
landed in Paris Charles DE Gaulle airport at 8:25 a.m.
twenty minutes behind schedule. Noticing Hans waiting at
the arrival gate, Anne quickly apologized to the tour group
director, telling him that she will join the group on the way
back as her family were there waiting for her. She then flung
herself into Hans's arms.

- How was your flight? Did you manage some sleep on the plane?
- No, I was too excited to sleep. I cannot believe that I am here and for two weeks.
- You must be exhausted. I will take you home. I mean to my flat.
- Your flat will be home for me Hans.

He put his arm around her waist as they dragged and then loaded her suitcase in his car.

No sooner had she entered his apartment, than she hugged and kissed him passionately dragging him to the bedroom. Like a person parched in the wilderness for a long time, she yearned to satisfy her sexual appetite. Fully relaxed and happy afterwards, she fell into a deep sleep.

Six hours later, he gently woke her up. She got up half naked, and sat on his lap.

- So how many women did you bring here ? she asked him with a mischievous smile.
- Three or four, if you want the truth. But I did not bring them, they brought themselves in. Rest assured, they left without getting what they came for. All because of you. I could picture you getting outrageously upset with me, so I sent them away.
- You naughty boy. I will force myself to believe you.
- My one and only love, let us discuss our program. Here is what I suggest. Tonight

I take you out for dinner. For the next five days, I will take you to visit museums, starting with my favorite Musee D'Orsay. I also booked one concert. Almost all concert halls and orchestras go on vacation in August, the only thing available is a jazz concert.

We will also walk along the Champs Elysée and visit various shops. I want to show you a Paris that the normal tourist does not see. I do not want to rush you. You need to get over the jet lag, so we will play it by ear. Then I want to drive you to Southern France, we can stop in Montpellier for a meal and rest, the wine is good there. We would then continue to Nice, where we can spend five nights. We can go swimming, drive to Mont Carlo for a visit, and on another time, visit other cities in the vicinity like Cannes and St. Tropez. I already made hotel reservations in Nice.

- That sounds wonderful Hans. I am so excited. What should I wear for tonight?
- Nothing fancy. I am taking you to a simple restaurant in the Montmartre area.

Montmartre is a favorite place for artists. The food is usually simple, but very good and the surrounding atmosphere is a bit bohemian. We leave around 7 p.m. In the meantime, I can offer you a small bite to eat with either a drink or a cup of coffee. I suggest you overcome the desire to go to sleep again.

Hans was right. The food was more than good. It was excellent, and the bottle of wine, he selected superb. No

71

comparison with the wine available at the liquor board in Toronto. Hans raised his glass:

— I drink to your beauty, elegance, and warmth.
— And I drink to our love.

He smiled and added:

— Do you know what I am thinking of now? A French song by Juliette Greco. In it, a man tells his lover, "I want to build you a big palace and buy you a dress studded with diamonds" and she answers him "I would be satisfied with a small studio overlooking the Seine River, and you in my bed". I mention this because on many occasions, that is how I felt. I wanted to give you the best in the world, a big house and everything you fancied. Since I could not afford it, I felt that I was not worthy of you. All this changed that fateful day at Toronto airport, when you found a place for me in your heart. He paused.
— I will always cherish and remember that day.
— I do not know when our love started. It has been growing more with each encounter. Something strange is happening to me Hans. I do not feel guilty about Jeff. Like your Katia, they are both nice and good people, but I guess you and I wanted different profiles that matched our own interests in life. We are so lucky to have found each other. Even if we are not living together as husband and wife or loving partners, my soul is wedded to yours and will always be. What does the woman in that French singer says at the end?

—   You in my bed.
—   That is what I want. Shall we go?

Anne's initial five days in Paris passed like a dream. Visiting the Louvre, the Musee D'Orsay, walking down the Champs Elysée and other major boulevards window shopping at times and real shopping at other times was overwhelming. Anne bought a swim suit from the printemps department store. Looking at the mirror while trying it on, she was no longer concerned about any imperfections in her body. Every day they went to various small restaurants, some offering French and others ethnic cuisines. The food was always good.

On the sixth day of her arrival, Hans drove her south. They stopped at Montpellier for lunch, explored the city and surrounding vine country, before continuing to Nice. The following several days were spent swimming and visiting picturesque villages where they also stopped for dinner or lunch. These included St. Paul de Vence, a 12th. century fortified village, home to painters, poets, and writers; the towns of Antibes- Juan-Les-Pins with its flowery old city, Vallauris, the French capital of pottery and ceramics and where Picasso once lived.

Along the French Cote D'Azur, Hans drove her to Mont Carlo, the small independent principality, where Grace Kelly was Princess. They went to St. Tropez with its pretty alleys, a tourists' playground. They visited Cannes, walked on its Corniche as they had done on the Nice Corniche. This latter corniche is commonly known as "La Promenade des Anglais". This name was forged early in the 20th. century when scores of British tourists used to flock to Nice and walk by its corniche.

Anne's time in France was now nearing an end.

— My dearest, I brought you these from the tourist office. They are brochures relating to Bretagne, Normandy, and Omaha Beach, and to the two Chateaus mentioned in your tour program. You can read them on the plane. If somebody asks you, on your return to Toronto, about your trip, you can then answer them and volunteer to show them these brochures.

— You think of everything, my love. This time spent together will be carved in my memory for life. I cannot find another excuse next year to come and be with you. That makes me very sad, very sad indeed.

— I will come to see you. Now that young Julie is studying in Montreal. I will come to see how she is doing at least once, if not twice a year. It will be easy for me then to get to Toronto for two or three days. In the meantime, we will continue to be in touch by phone.

— I know, but phone calls are no substitute to feeling your touch and your warmth.

Anne's trip back was uneventful. Jeff was particularly keen on knowing about her trip to Omaha Beach.

— Very sad to see all these graves of the US fallen soldiers., she said, the whole trip was very nice but tiring. I am glad I went. I brought you some brochures, if you want to look at them. I also have something for you. She produced a sport shirt and an accompanying light sweater.

Six months later, Hans was in town, having checked at a Toronto hotel for a couple of nights. They met at his hotel room, enjoying their intimacy. A year later, he was back again. Over lunch, they exchanged their news:

— Julie is doing fine, He told her, she is highly motivated and has consistently obtained high grades. She already applied to the McGill school of Nursing, a year ahead of time. As for him, he was promoted to a senior manager at work, supervising a team of junior staff. This is one level below being a partner.
— Jeff is not doing all that well. He now walks slowly, and I would say not too steady on his feet. I got him to use a walking stick. Paul made up his mind. He wants to go for electric engineering, and wants to do his Bachelor degree at Stanford in the US. His real interest lies in the emerging area of computer science. He feels that is where the future lies. I have encouraged him and bought him an IBM machine, which had just become available on the market. He says, apart from Engineering courses, Stanford also offered courses in information technology.
— You did well. There is quite a talk at the office about using computer technology to facilitate and improve our work in accounting. A task force was created to

> follow this lead, find out what others are doing and contact some computer providers to get to know more about this area. I am very happy about Paul and wish him all the best.

> — It is hard for me, not to have him around, but his future comes first. I am proud of him. He is growing up to be a mature person for his age, and well-rounded in the subjects you and I care about. If only you can meet him, but then I will have to reveal to him the extent of our relation.

Hans was silent for a while.

> — I guess you are right. Let us keep it at that my love.

Anne and Jeff now slept in separate beds. He had suggested it, given his sleep disorders, and she readily accepted it. For a while now, Anne felt that her stature at home, has changed, from a wife to a care giver. Hans was her real shadow husband. He gave her the love and affection she yearned for. She would soldier on in this stale marriage and seek overwhelming happiness with her true love whenever they met. Three years passed, before that fateful day. Jeff had gone out with his walking stick for the customary short walk outside their house, when he slipped over a small batch of ice that he had not noticed. He fell and could not move. Alone at the time, Anne tried lifting him but he was too heavy for her. An ambulance took him to a hospital. He had fractured his hip. Three days later, he passed away.

Hans asked Anne on the phone, if she would like him to fly over to be with her for the funeral. She gave him a categorical negative answer.

– Thank you, Hans. No. I want a respectable time to pass by, say three months or so, then I will come and spend time with you in Paris.

When Anne arrived in Paris, tired, relieved, sad, and happy all at once. Hans knew better, he gave her the time she needed to relax, before discussing their future, now that she was free.

Lying in bed, he asked her about her new mode of life, was she too lonely, how did Paul take this news, does she have any money worries, if that was the case, he was ready to step in. A year ago, he became a Partner at the company and was well off.

– Paul has one more semester to go before graduation. He is doing well at school and like me, expected this sad news to happen someday. He has been so close to me, far more than to his father, and now he has grown even closer. He said that after graduation, he will seek a job in Canada, rather than the US to be near me.

Financially, I found out that Jeff had taken a big life insurance, amounting to a million dollars, with a quarter of the sum due in case of unexpected death, going to Paul, and the rest to me. Since his death was due to an accident, that is his fall, and, as the policy was made with his own company, they did not put any hurdles and settled the matter rather quickly.

Hans turned, put his arm around her to bring her body closer to his.

- – Will you marry me, my darling.
- – I knew that this was coming, my love. I have been thinking about it for a while. I am sixty, and you are four years older. When people get married, they share their worries and unload their problems on each other. Be it job opportunities and career prospects, financial worries, family, friendship and even pet issues. Love may continue to be felt, but with some couples, it gradually fades into the background, ceding its place to daily problems. With others it may fade quicker, leaving nothing but mundane problems to replace it. At our age, we have no problems to worry about neither now or in the future. Our concern will relate mainly to our two children Paul and Julie. We will have a cherished past, but not much of a future to worry about. Our love for each other will always dominate our lives, whether we are married or not.

There is also another issue. Maybe I am imagining things, but if we get married now and if our relation is exposed, does this open the door for accusations that it was me who pushed my husband to his fall, so that I could marry you. The insurance company could even contest my claim.

Hans listened; her argument made sense. Nevertheless, he wanted to address the age issue.

– You know, my love, true we are in our sixties, but we are not old. I doubt that we will ever be. I have my own theory about aging. I think we grow old along three dimensions; the physical, the mental and the emotional. Not all three grow in tandem or at the same rate. We could in the years ahead grow weaker physically, but our mental ability may be only marginally impaired, and we could have the same emotional and physical attraction towards each other, as when we were in our thirties or forties. It is true what you say about our future worries. We will probably be speaking more about the past than about the future, so what?

If we do not get married, then I want to be near you. I cannot bear periods of long separation, anymore. Next year, I will turn sixty-five, a good time for me to retire.

I will spend my retirement years in Canada, where I can be with the two persons I love most in the world; you and Julie. Julie graduates this year. She told me she will be looking for a job in a smaller hospital. She does not want to be part of what she describes as a large efficiency-oriented organization, loaded with rules. and where she is just a cog in a fast -running machine. At a smaller hospital, she may be able to get to know better and devote more personal attention to every patient. Of course, you and I will travel together to Europe and other destinations whenever we want, but we will build our love nest in Canada.

A year later, Julie got a job at the Northumberland hospital at Coburg, Ontario. She described the little town by the lake to her father as charming and quiet. She found a nice house with an adjacent two-bedroom accommodation on the outskirts of town, overlooking the lake. They could live side-by-side if he agreed. Hans phoned his agreement without even seeing the place. It was ideal and not far from Toronto where Anne lived. He prepared to retire and leave Paris for good.

As soon as Hans settled in his new home, he wanted Anne to come and see it. She said she would do so, only if Julie is at work.

- But why? I want you to meet her.
- I prefer not to. Our relation has been plutonic, carnal, and clandestine, all three ! and I would like to keep it that way. It is exciting to keep meeting you in secret. It makes me feel like a teenager again. I love it that way Hans.

During the spring, they took a month-long trip together to the Far East. They could not stop in Cambodia because of the ongoing war there. The following year they took a trip to Europe. Hans was eager to see Germany after unification. They did. Then they went on to Paris, continued to Basel in Switzerland, and on to Austria. Their European tour ended in Italy, where they spent three days in Venice, and two days in Rome.

Two years later, they took a Nordic cruise to the Norwegian fjords, Tallin in Estonia, St. Petersburg in Russia, and Sweden's Stockholm.

It was a year or more, after their return from these trips, that Hans felt unduly tired. His sense of fatigue was coupled with a feeling that his heart was racing whenever he did any exercise. The insertion of a pace maker, carried out several months later, eased the problem. From there on, they decided to take life easy. They did simple enjoyable things, walking in parks, taking lake ferries, going to markets to shop for exotic tropical fruits, and other produce, exploring various ethnic restaurants in the city. Several years passed before Hans's sense of fatigue returned. He was diagnosed with partially blocked arteries. Four stents were needed to improve his blood flow. This was a routine operation, they were told.

Anne waited for a phone call from him a day after the operation, but it never came. When two days later she did not hear from him, she called him at home, there was no answer. She then called the hospital and received the news, she dreaded. Hans died shortly after the operation. A day later, she received a letter from Julie giving her the funeral arrangements.

Anne could not get herself to accept the sad news in Julie's note.

She cried her heart out for days. She hesitated, but then opted not to go to his funeral. She could not bear the sight of seeing him confined to a small grave, nor to see heaps of earth covering his body. Her life seemed to have come to an end as well. She no longer cared much for her appearance, lost her appetite. She had no more a desire to go for outings nor for lengthy walks, similar to what she did beore. Even Paul noticed this change in her. She assured him that she was alright. She just got sad news about the death of an old friend, but nothing serious. But clearly, she lost the will of wanting to live. Two years later, her wish came true. She was 72 years old when she died.

Chapter Eight

When Hans arrived in Paris for his new assignment, his ardent desire was to visit his country of origin, Germany, now divided between East and West. He was sixteen years old when he left Dresden. He could not go there now as it fell in East Germany, but he could well visit other places, in West Germany. It took him some time to fulfill his wish. He had to settle in Paris first, find a place to live for him and his family, a kindergarten for his four years old Julie and get himself and Katia accustomed to their new surroundings.

At first Kaia was curious about Paris, she enjoyed seeing several of its landmarks, but within months, this curiosity wore out. The realities of day to day living became trying. She found the shopping for food and other necessities vastly different from home. She thought the people lacked warmth, at times had little patience with foreigners, and were self -centered. She missed her favorite TV shows and as she hardly spoke the language, French TV programs were not a substitute. In addition, Katia could not see herself driving in Paris, nor in France generally where a driver needed to be both aggressive and defensive at the same time. Hans could do little to counter his wife's frequent complaints. He took the family for weekend drives outside the city, but after a couple of excursions, Katia showed no interest or desire to join him, on any more trips. When a year later, she left to Canada for medical treatment, Hans's anxiety over her health, were mixed with a sense of relief.

He took an advantage of a long weekend to fly to Berlin. This being his first return to Germany, since his younger days, he landed there excited and apprehensive at the same time. The war had been over for more than seventeen years by now. He did not know what to expect. Was he going to find a city scarred by ruined buildings, and pot marks on the walls? To his surprise, he did not notice anything reminiscent of the city's recent tragic past. The first impressions were good. Everybody spoke German, that generated a sense of belonging for him. Taking the subway, walking the streets, going to shops, he saw prosperity everywhere. No sign of the militaristic environment, that prevailed when he was growing up. Gone were with the Hitler youth and the Brown shirts parades. Instead, he saw many youngsters wearing blue jeans, several letting their hair grow down to their shoulders and even some with tattoos. The only military he saw, were US soldiers in uniform, and the occasional British and French soldiers loitering in bars or walking the streets. He went to the Brandenburg gate, where he could climb a platform and watch the East part of the city across the separating wall. The streets there, looked rather empty with very little traffic. He walked to "Check Point Charlie" saw a sign in English and German "You are now leaving the US Zone". His biggest disappointment came when he found out that the four major Berlin museums were now in East Berlin, and therefore were out of bounds for him. He longed having Anne with him. If she were, he would have opened up with her about his constant search for his identity. Was he still German, or Canadian or even French? Has his country of origin, changed from what he knew in his youth, or has he changed? He wondered if he would be happier to return and live in present day Germany.

He was glad he took that trip. He will visit Germany again, that is for sure. There were other cities to discover, Munich, Frankfort, Hamburg, and perhaps the day will come when he can also visit his city, Dresden.

Back in Paris, he immersed himself in his work, but also made time to explore the city, particularly over the weekends. The work itself was interesting, and provided a scope for him to do assignments in other French cities as well, such as Toulouse, Lyon, and Marseilles.

Other opportunities, of a different nature, presented themselves for him in Paris. Like cities elsewhere, many women, married, divorced or single were on the look for a partner; be it for one night, or for a longer duration. Several crossed his way. Some were female clients, others worked at his office, or were introduced to him at social gatherings. There were insinuations, outright proposals for a weekend spent together; and on a few occasions, some showed up unannounced at his flat. He resisted these temptations. For one thing, he respected the institution of marriage, even if Katia was away or did not fulfill his expectations. Second, as a methodic man, he always pondered the end, before the beginning. If he were to start a relation with one or another woman, can it end without a consequence? Then there was the emotional side. He dreamt of sex, as the culmination of a love that tied the two partners together, and not as an end in itself. Emotionally, he was tied to Anne and has been for years. She was his closest friend, the cultured intellectual person he could share his feelings with. Then there was her beauty. Her flowing black hair with blue eyes, her tiny nose, full lips, and an inviting body. He had desired her from the time he was a student in Montreal. Each visit that he paid her in Toronto brought him closer to her. It took him days, thereafter, to suppress his emotions. At the time, he had to face the facts. She was engaged elsewhere, and he got himself married in a hurry. So, while he was very much attracted to her, he had to face the realities of life.

When he returned with Julie after Katia's funeral, their meeting at the airport changed everything. There was a declaration of mutual love, together with their first kiss. He could dream of her without restraint or a feeling of guilt. What would it be like if she shared his life? Be the first person, he sees when he wakes up, and the last before he goes to sleep. What would love making with her be like? He could go on dreaming like this for ever.

For now, however, six years old Julie was in his care, and he wanted to give her the combined love of a father and a departed mother. He wanted to bring her up to be a cultured well- educated girl. He was determined not to be issuing instructions all the time, but to assume the role of a friend.

He wanted to encourage her to discuss with him everything that matters to her. He will share with her his love for the arts, for history, for current affairs, or anything else that comes to her mind.

A few months later, his resolve came to the test. Julie wanted to know how he and her mother met. Was it love at first sight; how did they decide to get married. Hans responded by saying that yes, it was love that motivated them to get married. He praised Katia a great deal, but then she asked him about untie Anne.

- What do you want to know?
- Is she going to replace Mommy?
- Why do you think so?
- I saw you kissing at the airport.
- I owe a lot to untie Anne. She found me a job when I came to Canada after the war, and helped me settle in that country. She is a wonderful lady.
- Dad, what did you do during the war?
- I was studying in Switzerland at the time. I did not go to war.

He knew that he was not telling her the whole truth, whether it was about Anne, or about his war years. but he preferred to leave it that way. She was too young to appreciate the whole truth.

Every weekend, he took Julie somewhere to explore Paris. There were museums to visit, concerts and music festivals to attend, and plays to see. There were also parks, markets, fun excursions and river boats to take. Julie loved it all. She adored her father. She was now fluent in French, and the international school she attended, kept her well-grounded in English as well. In addition, she also took German as an option. As she grew up, Hans often shared with her as he did with Anne, his views about world affairs.

His professional work in Cambodia, was an eye opener. He saw poverty, yet in that country, it was mingled with happiness. People were always smiling. They took their poor conditions in their stride. Children were playing in the streets often bare feet, sometime with an over worn tennis ball, many times under the rain, but they were giggling and sounded happy. Prince Sihanouk, even though, erratic at times, was a father figure to his people. It all sounded like one happy family. Hans felt an affiliation with that country. He kept an eye on whatever news he could get about Cambodia. In 1970, he was dismayed to read that the Cambodian chief of staff General Lon Nol staged a military coup that ousted Sihanouk. The general received massive US military support to suppress a grass roots communist movement, supported by China and Vietnam, known as the "Khmer Rouge" led by a certain Pol Pot. The American military were now involved in both Vietnam and Cambodia. Hans had no sympathy for the communists, who had divided and occupied half of Germany. His sympathy lay with the average Cambodian person caught in that fierce fighting, and with the deposed Sihanouk. Julie's reaction to Hans stories of Cambodia was sympathetic. She wondered if he or she could do something to help the poor people he described.

This sentiment may have also been fed by the events that took place in Paris. At the beginning of May 1968, a far-left student uprising took place leading to the occupation of universities. The students demonstrated against capitalism, consumerism, and traditional institutions. The high-handed police repression with raging battles in the streets, led to sympathy strikes organized by the unions. An estimated ten million workers went on strike, occupying factories across France. The work stoppage and the violence threatened the very existence of the French state. One of the most vocal leaders of the movement, and its spokesperson was in fact a German student, by the name of Daniel Cohn-Bendit. He came from a German family known for its communist sympathies, and arrived to study in France only three years earlier. Many people, and in particular students in various schools in France, like the one Julie was attending, showed sympathy for the demonstrators. For them, these were calls for the birth of a new society with a humanistic, rather than a materialistic face. The movement itself fizzled a month later when an agreement between the government, unions and employers led to significant gains for the workers, and when fresh elections were held, giving the Gaullist government in power, a large majority.

Hans had frequent discussions with his daughter during that upheaval about its root cause. He encouraged her to express her views while steering her away from extreme positions. Julie, now thirteen years old, wanted to contribute to a more humanistic society. Her idea of wanting a career at which she can help others was commendable. They began to explore the possibilities; a social worker perhaps. That did not appeal to her. A lawyer ? Many lawyers were more interested in making money than serving their clients, that is not what she wanted. A doctor? Perhaps, but it takes too long to study. Nursing? Why not. Contrary to north America, nursing education in France did not lead to a university recognized bachelor degree. It was then that she and Hans decided on her going to Montreal for a two years pre-university secondary education, (so-called CEGEP in Quebec), with the objective of joining the school of nursing at McGill University in Montreal after that.

Hans had another pre-occupation concerning his daughter. Leaving her alone in a big city like Montreal, at a tender age, can be risky. He sat her down one day with a glass of wine. He told her that as a father and a friend he had something to talk to her about.

— As you know, I always encouraged you to bring your friends home. On some occasions, you confined in me your likes and dislikes of certain boys. I was so happy when you did that. I think it is time for me to share with you my personal experience in that respect. During your stay in Montreal, you will meet other boys, you will fall in love or think you are. This is natural and a wonderful feeling, but always make a distinction between a person you love, and one with whom you may spend part of your life with. It is easy to fall in love, but it is difficult to find a person whose interests matches yours. You also need a person who can readily share with you every day's challenges, be it health, money or career problems. So, feel free to fall in love as many times as you want, but do not enter into any long-term commitments except after long reflection.

You asked me before about my married life. I met your mother when I was young, lonely and I had no clear prospects for a career. She came to Montreal to study and learn French. We met, readily fell in love, and got married rather quickly. It was only later, when we discovered that we were not a good match. Her interests in life were at variance with mine. This does not mean that my inclinations were better than hers or vice versa. It simply meant that we were frequently, at odds with each other. We never spoke of divorce or separation. It was a situation we accepted, unhappy as we were.

I had met Anne years earlier. I was new in Canada, alone and a lonely person seeking a place I could call home after the war ravaged my country of origin. She found me a job, showed a genuine interest in getting my news in case more help was needed. We met on occasions and gradually discovered our mutual interests. She got married to a nice person, but like me and Katia, her husband, did not meet her aspirations. His interests in life were vastly different from hers.

Nothing serious happened between Anne and me, until that time when you saw us kissing at the Toronto airport. That was when we first expressed our love for each other. Anne is not going to leave her husband for me. She respects the vows she took when she married him.

I want you to know the extent of my relation with Anne, dear Julie. What I can tell you is that we are both very happy when we get together, but, at present, it is like a story waiting for an end. When it comes to long term relationship, promise me that you will not repeat our mistakes. Mistakes that both Anne and I made when we chose our partners in life. I want you to be the happiest person on earth.

Julie bent over, hugged her father, and whispered in his ear; I promise. She added I am so happy you confided in me. You make me feel like a grown- up person. It will be hard for me to spend years away from you. I hope something happens between you and Anne. From now on I am calling her Anne, and dropping the untie. I wish I can meet her one day.

This discussion helped lift a burden off him. From now on, he does not have to conceal from his daughter, anything anymore, about Anne. When he took Julie to Montreal for her pre-University years, he was relieved to have found her, with the help of friends, a nice family to live with. Before leaving her, he made sure she had everything she needed. He told her he will be constantly in touch by phone. She was to call him at any time, and need not have a reason to do so. He will also come to Montreal once or twice a year to see her, and they will spend her summer vacation together.

Hans then turned his thought to the most wonderful event that awaits him. Anne's forthcoming visit to Paris. At first, he thought of taking her, on the first night, to one of those Michelin starred restaurants. A couple of days later, he changed his mind. He thought it would be better to take her to Montmartre, a favorite place for writers, painters, singers, and artists of all types. It boasted several good restaurants, nothing fancy, but good food, served in a rather friendly manner. They could then wander in the streets, looking at surrounding casinos, painters selling their ware, or listen to an accordion player performing on a pavement. That should be more appealing than being in a stuffy upper -class Michelin starred restaurant. That matter settled; he then turned his attention to sightseeing outside Paris. A visit to the tourist office, led him to the choice of the south of France. This offered the added opportunity to also visit quaint and historic villages and small towns in that region. Many of which, he had not seen himself. He soon finalized his plan and made the necessary hotel reservation in Nice for "Monsieur et Madame Hans Wien".

For as long as he lived, he will always remember those two weeks spent with Anne.

It was the fulfillment of a dream he had harbored for years. She was both sensual, intellectual and had a happy disposition. Both of them, had not had sex for a long time, and tried to make up for lost time. They talked, exchanged jokes, braved the sea waves holding hands and toasted each other at various restaurants. When it was time for her to part, he told her.

- Do you realize, we have not had a fight since you came.
- Why do you say that, were you wishing it ?
- Yes, because the best part is making up after a fight. Lovers' fights are quick to heal, but making up is

> always dramatic, sometimes full of tears, kisses and future promises.
> — Let us make up then without a fight, would that be agreeable?

That said, she held him tight.

Hans' life changed. It was all for the better. At work, he was promoted to a senior manager. He was now in charge of a team of junior accountants. His job required him to be in touch, and be available, even at short notice, to a specific number of clients. They could discuss with him their problems and needs, and he would suggest solutions.

Julie on the other hand completed successfully her high school studies and was admitted to the McGill school of nursing. She asked him if she can share an apartment with two student girlfriends during her university years. The apartment was walking distance from her school. He travelled to Montreal, invited Julie and her two friends to a good dinner. He saw the place liked it and signed the renting contract.

He then flew to Toronto for a couple of days, met Anne, this time at his hotel room. Their love for each other had grown stronger, Jeff was ailing, she told him.

It was becoming increasingly difficult for Anne and Hans to part company or to contemplate a life for one without the other.

Their relation took another turn, after Jeff's death. He asked her to marry him, but she had good reasons to want to keep their love above the daily issues often faced by married couples. Besides, they were now advanced in age. She could not see herself wearing a wedding dress at that age. Getting married when they were in their sixties could raise many eyebrows. There could be the inevitable curiosity about how long they had known each other. Some may question if that was a marriage of convenience. In addition, she was not also sure how her son Paul would take it.

At work, Hans, had now become a partner, with a good increase in his income. It came at a time in which he was contemplating retirement. He decided to soldier on for two more years.

They took three trips together, one to the far east, stopping in Bangkok to visit its several pagodas and the floating market, followed by a short stop-over in Hong Kong, then a ten days trip to Japan. They did the usual tourist trip, visiting Tokyo, Kyoto, and Nara. They attended a tea ceremony, went to a kabuki theatre, and enjoyed Japanese food. One thing struck Hans. Both Germany and Japan were occupied by the Americans after the second world war. However, in Germany, the younger generation began to adopt American attitudes, Jeans, long hair, tattoos, love of rock music, but here in Japan, people seemed immune to any cultural pollution, as he called it. They mostly kept to their traditions and values.

Their second trip together was to Europe. Apart from Paris, he wanted to go with Anne to Germany to visit it after unification. Apart from Berlin and Munich, they went to his former home town, Dresden. He tried to find his old family home, but could not locate it. Reconstruction after the massive bombing during the war had obliterated many city features, that he remembered. He was happy to find out that Dresden was home to some of the strongest resistance movements against the East German regime, particularly during the last two years of its existence. That visit severed whatever sentiment he had for that city. They then proceeded to Austria, stopping at Vienna, a city that still bore the marks of the old Austro-Hungarian Empire with its old castles, churches. Still, recent history left its mark as well, with such things as the café centrale, where Hitler, Stalin and Trotsky drank coffee at one time or another.

They went there for coffee and cakes. They had also booked and attended a concert at the Vienna Opera House. From Vienna they went to Salzburg. They planned their arrival to the city to coincide with the Mozart festival, where they attended chamber music concerts with the musicians dressed in seventeen century attires, on to the small beautiful city of Innsbruck, before leaving Austria to Switzerland, where Hans wanted to visit Basel where he had gone to university in his younger years. Foremost he visited his mother's grave. They took a train through the Swiss Alps to Lugano in the Italian part of the country, where they boarded another train to Milano and on to Venice. Walking over the many small bridges that crossed the various canals to St. Mark Square. visiting the Doge palace and the bridge of sighs was memorable. Their tour ended in Rome, with the colosseum, several water fountains, and the Vatican. From there they boarded a plane back to Toronto.

On their third trip, they opted for a Nordic cruise. It started in Bergen, Norway, on to Tallin, capital of Estonia with its charming old town, then to St. Petersburg, perhaps the most beautiful city in Russia and even in Europe, overlooking the Neva River, historic buildings like the Hermitage, one of the top museums in Europe, the church of the blood, one of the most beautiful in Russia which got its name because the grandfather of the last Tsar, was assassinated there, as he left that church, the Peter and Paul cathedral where the Romanovs, Tsars of Russia are buried. There were also other buildings of historic interest like the palace of Prince Yussupov, where Rasputin was murdered. Unfortunately, the cruse guided tour did not accommodate all these sights on their wish list. They felt that the visit to that city was too short, they decided that they would return on another occasion. The cruise then continued to the beautiful city of Stockholm, where they took a sightseeing tour on a ferry, the city itself being spread over a few major islands.

These last two trips were taken after Hans's retirement. He now lived beside his daughter in Cobourg Ontario, where she was a nurse at the local hospital. With time,

Hans began to gradually feel the weight of the years. There were no more talks of long trips overseas. He suffered the usual pain in one knee, his pace slowed down and he developed a slight stoop of his shoulders. More significant, was his sense of fatigue and some chest pain. A pace maker improved his condition dramatically. He resumed his normal activities with Anne, walking the parks, Lake Ontario boat trips, driving to the thousand Islands and visiting Ottawa and its art gallery.

Three years later, when his fatigue returned, he was diagnosed with partially blocked arteries. The operation of putting four stents was a routine, non- evasive surgery. Doctors performed such an operation hundreds of times, he was told. Just before going to the hospital, he scribbled a note to Anne. In the operating room, three stents were introduced successfully. However, on introducing the fourth stent, a blood clot blocking the blood flow and stuck to the artery wall, became loose, when the artery was widened to make a place for the stent. In a split second, that clot travelled to the brain and blocked the flow of blood there. Hans went into a coma, was paralyzed. A day later he was declared dead. He was 76 years old.

Chapter Nine

Julie opened the hand- written envelope addressed to her. It was very unusual for her to receive a letter at her place of work. Most probably, it was from someone enquiring about a patient in her care. If so, she will refer it to the concerned doctor. She quickly glanced at the signature. "Paul". She did not know anybody by that name.

12 June 1994

Dear Julie,

My name is Paul. I am the son of Anne Hamilton. My mother passed away a couple of weeks ago. It was then that I discovered that she was close to your late father. Should you know better about their relation, and should your time permit it, I would very much like to meet you and exchange information about our parents.

I can drive from Toronto to Cobourg on a weekend, and meet you for that purpose.

I would be very happy if I can host you for a lunch or dinner at a restaurant of your choosing in the city. I would be equally happy, if your husband or your friend can join us, if you think this is appropriate.

I found out your address at the hospital from a letter you addressed to my mother announcing your father's death, some two years ago. Can you please phone me at this number 416-223-2943. I can be reached after 7 p.m. during the week, or on the weekends.

Sincerely,
Paul

Julie, read the letter once more. She had always been curious about Anne and her family. She knew from her late father that Anne had one son, which she adored, called Paul. She would love to meet him. Perhaps he can tell her more about his mother. She called him that same evening. A date was set at a quiet restaurant in Cobourg. She told him she will be alone and will be dressed in a blue blouse.

Paul arrived earlier, and was happily surprised to see a good-looking woman wearing a blue blouse, approaching his table. He stood up.

– Julie, I presume. I am Paul.

They did not know how to salute each other. A handshake, a waive or a bow. They settled for a handshake.

She was the first to start the conversation:

– I am sorry about your mother. I only found out from your note. Had I known earlier, I would have come to her funeral.

– Thank you. Did you know my mother?

– Unfortunately, no, but I know of her. My late father spoke a lot about her. He was very fond of her, and he did not hide his feelings from me. My father and I were very close and he treated me like a trusted friend.

– Tell me more about him. I only discovered his existence a couple of weeks ago.

– How?

– I found letters written by him to my mother. My mother kept their relation to herself.

– Do you still have these letters? I would love to read them. I too found letters written by Anne to him, but as I mentioned in a letter to Anne, I disposed of them.

My father was the most wonderful man, you can imagine. I think he was struggling with his identity all his life. He was born and raised in Germany, he lived there till the age of sixteen, went to Switzerland for studies, then to Canada during WWII. I am not too sure how this happened. Later, he became a Canadian citizen. He worked in Canada, then left to Paris for work and lived as much, if not more in France, than in Canada. So, there you have it, nationality-wise he was a German and Canadian, but culturally he was also, French.

At this point they were interrupted by the waiter. They ordered lunch, a bottle of wine and a bottle of mineral water. Julie resumed:

— In addition, my father was always trying to reconcile his moral upbringing, and high ethical values that he possessed, with the imperfections of the real world, where the ends justified the means.

My own mother died young, of breast cancer in Canada. I was barely four years old, when I accompanied her during her medical treatment in Winnipeg. Two years later, after her death, my father brought me back to Paris. He wanted me to be the happiest person in the world. He attended to many of my wishes without allowing me to be a spoilt brat.

On our first Xmas together, he took me to the Paris Opera to see the Nutcracker ballet. I was elated; thrilled by the story, and amazed at the dancers' talent. Two months later, he surprised me by taking me to another performance. It was the Swan Lake ballet. Again, I was amazed at the dancers' performance. Noting that infatuation, he asked me if I wanted to learn to dance like those that I saw on stage. Of course, I said yes. He subsequently enrolled me in the three months, summer course of the ballet school of the National Opera of Paris. I did this for two consecutive summers.

— You can dance ballet ? That is fantastic. My mother took me three times to watch performances by the National Ballet of Canada. I was really thrilled as well, but never dreamt of being a dancer myself. What happened after that?

- The courses could have led to a professional career in dancing, but that is not what I wanted. My father was a very humanistic person, and it rubbed on me. He felt for other persons problems and was always ready to offer a helping hand, if he could. I wanted to be like him in that respect. Now tell me about Anne.

- Thanks to my mother, my upbringing, I can say, is almost a copy of yours. My mother's aim was to have me not only educated, but also cultured. At an early stage of my life, she took me to ballet performances, to concerts and on several occasions to attend Shakespeare's plays at Stratford in Ontario. I loved them all. She also took me to visit the Art Gallery of Ontario, in Toronto, to see the paintings of the group of seven Canadian artists. Paintings done during the period of 1920-1933.

- Very interesting. Although I have been to many museums in Paris, including the most famous like the Louvre and D'Orsay, I have not been to the Art Gallery in Ontario, and I am not familiar with the work of the Group of seven. I heard a lot about the Stratford plays, but never seemed to have found the time to go.

- We both have our excuses. I wanted so much to go to Stratford next week to see

Shakespeare's "Taming of the Shrew", but I hated going alone, and used that as an excuse. If you are not engaged, and manage to find the time, you would be doing me a favor by accepting to be my guest. Stratford is not far. Have you ever been there?

- No. By the way I am neither married, nor engaged.
- Then please say yes, and I will see if I can get tickets right away. Stratford in Ontario was conceived to be a look alike to Stratford England, albeit with a Canadian touch. It is a small town by a river. We can have an early dinner there and then go to the theatre. And by the way, I too am neither married, nor engaged.

Julie thought it out for a minute, then added:

- O.K. why not.
- splendid. If I manage to get tickets for either Saturday or Sunday, then can you drive to Stratford, and we meet there, or do you prefer to drive to Toronto, where we can go together in my car.
- I think it would be easier if I drive straight to Stratford and we meet directly at the restaurant.
- Let us plan on giving ourselves two hours before the show for a leisurely meal. Give me your home phone number, and I will phone you this evening to confirm our tickets and the place where we will meet. I take it that either Saturday or Sunday will be O.K. with you.
- Yes.

With this settled, the discussion then drifted to the life in Coburg in comparison to big cities like Toronto and Montreal. That same evening, Paul rang her. No possibility of getting tickets this weekend, he told her, but there were some available two weeks later. He went ahead and bought two tickets and hoped that was alright with her. For this coming weekend, would she consider going to the Art Gallery in Toronto, as well as to the nearby Royal Ontario Museum. They could have lunch somewhere in the city. Would Saturday be agreeable to her. It was. He reserved at a Lebanese restaurant in the city.

When visiting the Toronto art galleries, Paul was impressed by the comments Julie made about some of the paintings. These could have come only from a connoisseur of art. She told him she was very happy to have discovered the works of Canadian artists. She had been immersed in European art, particularly the Impressionists, as her father took her to various museums in France, often explaining the history and nuances of many of these paintings. Paul told her, that impressionist's paintings were not as abundant in Canada as they were in Europe, that his art education, came from art books his mother showed him.

When they sat down for lunch, Paul explained that he chose that restaurant because of Anne's Syrian origins. Occasionally, she would prepare a Lebanese meal at home often claiming that it was not as good as her mother's, he added.

- Tell me Julie, how did you decide on a nursing career.
- It was a subject my father and I discussed together When I was as young as thirteen years old. At that age, one is invariably idealistic, often wants to save

the world, by serving the causes of the poor, the dispossessed, the sick and the refugees. You get that feeling more, living in Europe than in North America. Though my father's sentiments were aligned with mine, through discussions, he brought me down to real life from cloud seven where I floated. His feelings towards the less fortunate were genuine, but he cast the solutions in practical terms. He felt for people who suffered, and sometimes I felt that he shared their anguish. I do not know where this came from. Was it something he experienced during the war, or was it his exposure to the situation in other less developed countries. I have no clear idea as to his experiences during the second world war. He always gave me an evasive answer, and did not want to talk about it; but I can tell you about his reaction after he went on a mission to Cambodia.

— As for Hans's experience during the war, Julie, I can fill you in, on that.

— Are you serious? How did you find out?

— He confided in Anne, and she recorded it in her diary. You should be proud of your father Julie.

— Please Paul, tell me everything you know, the suspense is too much for me.

— Hans was brought up to hate the Nazis and everything they stood for, his father, a well- known physicist, died long before the war. With the rise of the Hitler Youth movement, his mother was worried that he may be put under pressure to join them. At the age of 16, she sent him for university studies in Switzerland. Hans wanted to do more to contribute

to the fall of the Nazi regime in Germany. At 18
years, and a few days before the outbreak of the war,
he abandoned his studies and enlisted in the French
Foreign Legion, which accepts all nationalities, no
questions asked. Although the war was declared on
the second of September 1939, actual hostilities,
when Hitler invaded Holland and Belgium and
attacked France, did not start except six months
later. During that time, Hans finished his military
training, was assigned to a regiment of the Legion,
which was dispatched to Algeria. After the collapse
of the French army in June 1940, an armistice
was declared and a French Government formed
stationed in Vichy, which nominally controlled half
of France; the other half put under direct German
rule. As you probably know, De Gaulle, had escaped
to England and established the Free French army
to continue the fight. I am sure you know all
that. What you, perhaps, do not know is that the
various French garrisons stationed in the French
colonies had to choose their allegiance; to the Vichy
government, or to the Free French of De Gaulle.
The Algerian regiment where Hans served chose
the Vichy government. That was against what Hans
had enlisted for, so he escaped to England, to join
the Free French. There, the British arrested him,
because he was German. His pleas that he wanted
to fight the Nazis and enlist in the free French army,
went nowhere. He was put in a German prison
camp and later shipped to Canada.

Julie was overwhelmed by emotions. She could imagine the suffering her father endured, all done to uphold his beliefs. Why did he keep this away from her? He must have felt terrible that the mission he set out to accomplish, that is fighting the Nazis, ended up a failure, with him being identified as one of them, taken prisoner in a war at which he did not fire a single bullet. Not much of a story to be proud of telling your daughter.

- Julie, you started saying something about Hans's experience in Cambodia.
- My father went twice to Cambodia. It was his first experience going to a least developed country. The first time, he spent slightly less than two months in that country. He was auditing the accounts and finding out what improvements he can make in the accounting system of the Michelin Rubber company there. Despite the poverty, he found people to be rather happy with a ruling Prince, who communicated directly with his people through the radio, on anything that came to his mind, even confidential news about his own family.

When he went back six months later for a short trip, he was caught in an upheaval, as the Americans had bombed a Cambodian village, presumably on a Vietcong trail. The Americans, at the time, claimed it to be a pilot error. There were riots in the streets and burning of so-called Anglo-Saxon properties. Somehow this experience marked him, and since then, he followed Cambodian news. He was a bit dismayed when he heard of a military coup that ousted

Prince Sihanouk. It seems that he was unable to deal with a grass roots communist insurgency called the Khmer Rouge, led by Pol Pot. Massive US military assistance followed, but twelve years later, the capital Pnom Penh fell to the Khmer Rouge.

My father was shocked when he heard the news that followed. He explained the situation to me and I am sure, he must have also shared it with Anne. The first order of the day of Pol Pot was to liquidate ethnic minorities. This included ethnic Chinese and Vietnamese often second or third generation Cambodian born. All the so-called intellectuals, were also liquidated. By intellectuals, were meant anybody who spoke foreign languages or had an education beyond elementary school. One day after entering the capital, Pnom Penh, everybody in the city, was ordered to leave their homes, and to start walking for days, sometimes weeks, to the countryside to work the land. That included the sick in the hospitals. Those who could not make it, were shot. All this was reported in the media. Over the years, many died of disease, malnutrition or were shot for one reason or another. Some two million or one third of the population perished, and Pnom Penh became a ghost town.

My father was so devastated by what was happening there, and wondered about the fate of the various persons he had met there. In the meantime, neighboring Vietnam had fallen to the communist Vietcong. It took another fourteen years, for these excesses in Cambodia, to be stopped by an invasion from another communist regime, that of Vietnam. The Khmer rouge retreated to the north west corner of the country fighting a ferocious battle to preserve their control of the Rubies mine. Finally, they were eliminated in 1998, six years after my father died. He would have been relieved had he heard this news; but it was not to be.

All these atrocities influenced my father's approach to life. He felt that the world needed to be more human, and he invariably transmitted that feeling to me. I grew up, with an ardent, desire to seek a career at which I can be of assistance to others. Now tell me about yourself.

– Nothing much to tell. I grew up, a curious person, inclined to try and solve problems, whenever I could. During the last couple of years of my secondary education, home computers came on the market for the first time. They aroused my curiosity. Developed for home use in the 1960's, by IBM, they were rare and clumsy at first, but my mother wasted no time in buying me one, as a Xmas present.

I wanted to learn more about them and about their use, so I made enquiries about universities that taught subjects dealing with computers. Two universities stood out at that time. They offered courses in computer science, without leading to a formal degree in that subject. These were the MIT and Stanford. I applied to both, got accepted by Stanford. Four years later, I graduated in electric engineering with a major in information technology. I was proud of that achievement, but all along, my mother kept reminding me that there were lots of people in this world who were, as much, or more educated than me. Few however, were both educated and cultured. This is what I aspire you to be, she would say. I want you to be able to accumulate enough knowledge across the board, that would allow you to discuss intelligently a variety of subjects, rather than the only one you acquired during your formal education. To that end, she devoted a good deal of time to making me appreciate subjects such as history, art, national and international social and political affairs.

She introduced me to classical music by delving into the life of a composer before hearing his composition. That way I was able to appreciate it more. We discussed some poetry as a prelude to attending the Shakespeare plays at Stratford. We visited museums talked about painters and went through catalogues of Dutch, Italian and Spanish classical painters, as well as those of the impressionists.

— You did not mention your father.
— My father was a very nice quiet man. He was in the insurance business. His job often took him away on business trips either to assess claims or to promote insurance policies. With me, his main interest was to follow my scholastic grades, to enquire about my career aspirations. He rarely discussed with me the subjects that my mother was keen on. I rarely saw him, if ever, taking my mother to a play or a concert. In his spare time, he enjoyed reading newspapers and watching TV. So, my mother, had far more influence on my upbringing than my father. Now come to think of it, I would say that although he and my mother rarely ever quarreled, their interests in life did not coincide.

To go back, after graduation, I was hired by an engineering consulting company. That company was active in introducing its clients to computer aided design, a tool that was available since the mid 1950's, and were now eager to move into computer aided manufacturing. This does not really match my interests.

- So, what do you propose to do. Will you stay with them or seek a job elsewhere and in that latter case, to do what.

- I have not told this to anybody, but I will share it with you. I am thinking of striking it on my own. I think the use of home- made computers will expand greatly in the years to come. The users may feel lost at the beginning, they may need help. I could guide them in that respect. The same could happen to companies, if computer use becomes widely spread, as I suspect, then I could also offer my services to the companies that want to use them. In other words, I would be a free lance consultant in the computer business.

- I think it is a great idea. It combines both your interest and looks like a sound money earning proposition.

- How about you Julie. Are you happy where you are.

- I am happy, but sometimes I feel I reached my limit. I would like to further my education by getting a master degree in Nursing. It is a one-year full time program. That means that I will have to resign my present job, if I go that way

When they left the restaurant, Paul suggested that they stop by his place, so that he can lend her Hans's letters to his mother. She asked if she could also borrow Anne's diary. She promised to return them when they met the following weekend at Stratford. Julie admired Paul's house.

- It is in a nice residential area and quite a big house.
- It is too big for me. I am alone now. Come I want to show you something.

He led her to Anne's room, opened the drawer and handed her Hans's letters and Anne's diary.

- My mother spent a lot of time in this room. She called it her sanctuary. Maybe, if I start my private business; I will make this room my office.

When Julie came to leave, she gave him a tiny kiss on one cheek.

- Thank you for the lunch, for a lovely day and for lending me these precious letters.
- You will notice that both the diary and the letters stopped after a certain date. They probably, continued their contacts by telephone.
- I am sure they did.

No sooner Julie had arrived home, than her telephone rang. It was Paul. He wanted to make sure she arrived safely. What a thoughtful man, she said to herself, and on top of that, he is good-looking, educated, and cultured. She looked forward to their next get together.

Chapter Ten

Paul looked forward, with great anticipation to his next date with Julie. He enjoyed her company. She was different from the various women he had dated before. A north American girl, with a European flavor, having spent several of her formative years in France. She was not one for small talk. One could have an easy dialogue with her on many subjects. Then there was her elegance, perhaps due to the six months ballet training, and her physical attraction. She was not only beautiful; she was also attractive, in fact very attractive. Always well dressed and groomed with a nice smile.

Paul began to ponder the possibilities. Should he cultivate this relation, but to what end? A love partner? He did not think she was the type of a person who would entertain such a relationship. A prospective wife? But he gave up on marriage after his failed first try. It was perhaps premature to think of an attachment since neither of them knew much about the other. She does not know yet, that he is a divorced man and he does not know if she has men in her life.

When they sat for a meal at the Thai restaurant in Stratford, he discreetly asked her about her personal experiences with men.

—　During my university years, I went out dancing and socializing like everybody else. These were fun years, nothing serious. I suppose you begin to think of marriage or starting a family, later, when you start working, or beyond a certain age. By then, you do not only want a lover, but a person with whom you can share and seek advice on a multitude of issues; your career aspirations, your financial worries, whether you want to raise a family early or later, and so on.

—　So, what happened when you started working?

—　As a young nurse, I was elated at first, when a young doctor asked me out. I went out with him on two or three occasions. I then discovered the obvious. When that person took off his white coat, which at work symbolized some authority, he became like everybody else. With that authority, he had over me at work, gone, I could fathom his character more clearly. It was easy to find out, that he was looking for an intimate relation with no commitments. That is not what I wanted.

—　Did you repeat that experience with other men?

—　I went out with a few, but none of them lived up to the promise I made to my father.

—　What was that?

—　That I would not enter in any long-term relation; marriage or otherwise, unless our interests in life matched. Look at our parents. Whether it is Anne or Hans, they both married nice persons, thought they were in love at the time they exchanged their vows. Later they discovered that what one of them liked, was of no interest to his or her partner. Their interests, whether in art, history, international affairs did not match. When Hans met Anne, their love for each other was sustained by their common interests in life. Now tell me about you.

— What you said is very true. I made the same mistake like my mother and your father. I thought I was in love in my early twenties, got married in a hurry. Divorce followed two years later. That experience affected me badly. Ever since, I have been trying to figure out what went wrong, and who was to blame for this failure.

The way you, and Hans before you, explained it, puts my mind at ease. It was neither party's fault. We were simply not matched, when it came to what we wanted from life

— You know Paul, one learns a great deal from one's own mistakes. I am sorry that you went through this experience. But I also believe, that it made you a more mature person.
— Julie, one more thing I want to mention and I hope you would not take offense.

Long before his death, my father, took a life insurance for a million dollars. He stipulated that in the case of his death, I get a quarter of that sum, and my mother gets the rest. As you know, she died a few years after him, so I find myself inheriting a big fortune. If you need to quit work, to get your master's degree, I will be more than happy to finance it. Our parents were friends, we are friends, and if this proposition bothers you, take it as a loan, with no interest, and with a clause that allows this loan to be forgiven, on demand.

— You are very sweet Paul. I think I can manage on my own. But you know, our parents were not just friends. Having read the letters you lent me and Anne's diary, it is obvious that they were deeply in love. Their long- lasting and fervent love for each other should be an envy to everyone. For your sake and mine, I wish we can develop the same feelings, towards prospective partners, like them.

******

Shakespeare's play "The taming of the Shrew", was delightful. It was witty and although it was written, four decades earlier, some of its propositions, could be relevant at present. When Paul walked her to her car, she tucked her arm under his. As he bid her goodbye, he gave her a kiss on one cheek. She reciprocated by giving him a kiss on the other cheek, saying with a giggle:

— In France, you kiss both cheeks.

On arrival home, she waited for a call from Paul. It came fifteen minutes later. Yes, she arrived safely, and like him she enjoyed that outing very much. He was right, she told him, they should go to Stratford more often.

That evening and the discussion they had, kept each of them awake for a while. Though far apart, they were both asking the same question. Are they gradually falling in love with each other. One thing was certain. They wanted to meet more often. Paul phoned her two days later, simply to tell her he wanted to hear her voice. He talked about various things, but not what she hoped to hear. A day later, he called again with some news. He gave his notice at work. Will leave at the end of the month to start his own business as she encouraged him to do. She congratulated him and wished him well.

- How about you will you go for the Master degree?
- I have been seriously thinking about it. Our discussion helped. I am gathering information of what is on offer in various universities.
- You need only to consider one, the university of Toronto.
- Why ?
- So that we can be near each other. By the way Julie, I am trying to find out something. Do you think we are a good match?
- Moderately so. She giggled. She thought that their relation was becoming a bit serious.
- Then I have to work hard at it, he answered.

Paul found himself attracted so much to her. He wanted to see her more often. For a few months, they met on several weekends. They exchanged views on many topics.

He told her, that much to his regret, he had not been to Europe. She went on to describe to him life in Paris, adding that he should probably go there for his honeymoon. He tried to explain to her his apprehension of getting married again.

He was worried that may be, he cannot make his future wife happy.

- Paul. You have to get over it. Start with a new slate. It all depends on finding a person, who is not only loving but who has a similar disposition to life like you.

The more Paul thought about it, the more he was sure that Julie was the person, he would dearly like to share his life with. He was attracted to her in every way, her beauty, her personality, her loving nature, and she also spoke her mind freely, like his mother. He wished he could be with her all the time. They did talk often on the phone, but he wanted more. He is definitely in love.

While deep in thought, one day, the phone rang, it was Julie.

- Paul. We need to talk, there is something important that I want to ask you. Can we meet at the cemetery?

Paul thought the meeting venue a bit odd, but he agreed. They met the following day.

- I want to confess to an incorrect statement, I relayed to both you and Anne. I told you that in accordance with my father's wishes, I destroyed all Anne's letters to him. That is not true. I could not. I put them with him in his coffin. I wanted theses letters to accompany him to the next world.

She paused for a couple of minutes.

– I now want to ask you this. Do you think it is fair to have Hans and Anne separated in death as they were in life. Would you consider having Anne's ashes re-buried in my father's grave. That way they can be together again now and in the afterlife.

Paul, struggled to contain a tear in his eyes.

– But of course, we should bring them together. Let us go to the office and see with them if this is feasible, and attend to whatever formalities are needed.

At the cemetery office, they were told, that exhuming a body can only be authorized by a court order, but in this case, since it is simply burying an urn, containing the ashes of a deceased in another grave, they could arrange it. There is paper work to be done, and fees to be paid. Paul said he will defray all expenses, but that he had two additional requests:

He wants to bring a small metal box containing intimate documents belonging to the departed, to be buried with her at the same time. Secondly, he wants the office to plant a bed of red roses by the grave. He also wants to subscribe to the maintenance of the grave site including the flowers. A date was then set for that reburial; two weeks later.

– What is this metal box you want buried Paul?

– It contains Hans's letters to my mother.

They walked out of the office in silence, hand in hand.

– This has been such an emotional experience Paul. Can we go to your house for a while. I do not feel like going anywhere else. I want to be alone with my thoughts and with you.

When they arrived home, he poured her a drink, fetched one for himself and sat beside her on the sofa in his mother's sanctuary. Few minutes passed before he put the question to her.

– I am in love with you Julie. Do you think we can get married, and have a happy life together. Do I live to the promise you made to your father? Do I match your expectations.

Her lips found his, for a passionate kiss.

– We are a good match. My father will be happy that I am fulfilling my promise to him. My mother too, she called me Juliette so that I can find my Romeo one day. You are my Romeo.
– In addition, we will be carrying our parents love for each other, to the next generation.
– Mind you, that will come with a great sacrifice on my part, I will have to change the Wien name, that of a great scientist, for Hamilton, a name invented by an immigration officer.

They both laughed, and decided that this was not the time to discuss the details of any forthcoming wedding. It was a day for celebration, for enjoying to the full their love for each other.

They went to the Mount Pleasant Cemetery on the designated date, each carrying a red rose. They watched as the urn containing Anne's ashes together with the box containing Hans's letters were lowered in Hans's grave. Paul kissed his flower and threw it in the open grave. Julie did the same, adding:

—   Our two dearests, united at last. We have come to tell you that we are getting married, will spend our honeymoon in Paris, following your steps. We will carry on your flame of love. Of this, rest assured and rest in peace.

Acknowledgement

Weaving a story with a Canadian background would not have been possible without a help from Georgette, my late wife. As a Canadian, she introduced me to the way of life in her country and to some of her friends who figure out in this novel. For that I will be eternally grateful.

To move from a manuscript to a published novel, I want to express my gratitude to the i Universe publishers' team, who accompanied me on this journey and in particular to Ellie Go, Fatimah Garrison and Eric Saxon.

Printed in the United States
by Baker & Taylor Publisher Services